WRENFERN
PUBLISHING

Copyright © April 2019 – 2024 E. Thomas King

The Author asserts the moral right to be identified as the author of this work.

Cover illustrations Copyright © August 2024 Karol King Woodroffe

Artwork Copyright © August 2024 Karol King Woodroffe

All rights reserved. No part of this publication may be reproduced, stored in a retrieval system, or transmitted in any form or by any means, electronic, mechanical, photocopying, recording, or otherwise, without the prior permission of the copyright owner.

This is a work of fiction. All characters and events portrayed in this book are fictitious and intended to be period accurate or are from the author's imagination and any resemblance to real persons, living or dead, is purely coincidental.

ISBN - 13:   978 1 068 52101 0

First published in the United Kingdom in 2024 by Wrenfern Publishing.

TOO STRONG TO DIE

CHAPTERS

1ST.	THE BEGINNING.	1
2ND.	VISITORS.	5
3RD.	GOING HOME.	15
4TH.	GROWING STRONGER.	23
5TH.	TARANTULA.	31
6TH.	GOING TO TOWN.	37
7TH.	DON'T BANK ON IT.	47
8TH.	MIMI AND ME.	61
9TH.	WAYNE MORGAN.	73
10TH.	GET A ROOM.	87
11TH.	JUDGE WOODROOF.	103
12TH.	INITIATION.	115
13TH.	PASSED THE TEST.	127
14TH.	INTO THE FUTURE.	141
15TH.	A SPIRITUAL JOURNEY.	161
16TH.	MADNESS!	177
17TH.	CONSPIRACY.	189
18TH.	VINCENTE.	203
19TH.	THE MEXICAN.	215
20TH.	THE LIEUTENANT.	229

CHAPTER 21. IN CONTENTION, IN CONTEMPT.	
	243
22ND.	THEY SAY YOU SHOULD NEVER GO BACK. 251
23RD.	TO THE MOON AND BACK! 265
24TH.	HOMEWARD BOUND. 281
25TH.	OLD MAN NOLAN. 293
26TH.	CHAPTER. THE NEW MARSHAL. 298

CHAPTER 27. DISCOVERING SENIOR DELGADO.
....309

CHAPTER 28. BETTER THAN THE ONLY REMAINING ALTERNATIVE. 315

CHAPTER 29. WAITING FOR A WOLF. 323

CHAPTER 30. A LEAVE OF MY SENSES. 333

CHAPTER 31. TO KILL OR NOT TO KILL. 341

CHAPTER 32. REMORSE. 349

CHAPTER 33. THE BEGINNING OF THE END. ..355

CHAPTER 34. COYOTE STEALS FIRE. 367

CHAPTER 35. ONE LAST JOB TO DO. 375

CHAPTER 36. THIS IS THE END! 385

36.25. ERROR! NOT FOUND. 393

36.5. THERE CAME A BEAR! 407

36.75. FULL CIRCLE. 411

1ST.   THE BEGINNING.

Can't say how old I am, I remember when my mother died. I had just started working the land with my father that spring. She passed in the fall of that same year. My father told me he was younger than most boys when he had become strong enough to work, I think he was proud of that. He had the same look on his face when I became strong enough and subsequently began to work the hard, dry land. No doubt due to the fact that I was even younger than he had been those many years ago, I dare say he was proud of that also. Since most boys begin work when they are 10, I guess I was somewhere between 8 & 10 when my mother died.

I worked with my father for 2 full seasons. He died in the winter of that second season not long after we had finished building the bull shed. The winter just passed will have been the 9th since he died

and I carried him all the way up to the ridge to bury in the shade under the great rock as he had done with my mother those few seasons before.
In conclusion to these events and the subsequent time passed, it would be my best guess to say that I am somewhere between 19 & 21 years.

      Still young in terms of the short years that I have been alive but by no means a young man in the same way that those young men in town are. We can hardly be compared, nor the lives that we have led. Most of those men have never been far from town or been without food or water for a period of time often as long as days. Many of those young men do not stray far from the whorehouse, only ever to find themselves at the saloon. It sounds like a good life for a young man, to a point. A life I would no doubt have enjoyed also, had it not been that my father died when I was still just a boy. As it is, life so far, has not been a good one. Was for a short time, whilst my mother was alive. Things got worse after she died, then again when my father died.

I quickly discovered that life was about endurance.
From that perspective at least, I had been thus far successful, given that I had endured these past 9 seasons and I have endured quite a lot.
Fever, disease, dehydration and starvation.
Sleep deprivation, extreme cold, extreme heat, poison and venom.
I have been beaten, raped, shot and cut.
Broken and bled, cheated, deceived and abandoned.
Besides more tormented, humiliated and pitied.
Above all else, by far the hardest to endure was pity.

2ND. VISITORS.

Not long after my father died a group of men came up to house on horseback. Can't say how they had known but somehow the news of my father's death had made it into town. As I recall I had somehow known they had come to claim my father's land for themselves, with him being gone it was only a matter of time before someone came. My father had a 6 acre ranch with a large house, the view in every direction was of the hard land touching the sky. 18 cattle, 2 barns, 4 horses and a whole bunch of tools. It was a treasure just waiting to be found, just waiting to be claimed.

When they came I was trying to repair the fence on the far side of the cattle pasture where it had been previously broken by the bull, the same bull that had killed my father the winter before last. He was a real bastard, almost as tall as my father was when sat on horseback, father had boasted in years past of the bull being almost 1000lbs. The bull had been a prize winner at the fair a long time ago, even before he was fully grown. It had been somewhat coveted ever since. Father had made the decision to stop taking him to the fair the year before my mother died, on account of he had become uncooperative and refused to be handled. Father did try shooting him at one time, it seemed to have little effect however. His character had gotten gradually worse in the following years, to the point that he had killed one of the cattle in favor of breeding with it.

    After that father stopped introducing the bull to the herd and it had to be kept in isolation, hence the bull shed. I was present when my father died and remember it clearly. He had gone into the shed for one reason or another, what that reason was I will never know. I am also unclear about the events leading upto the incident. Somehow he had been compressed between the bull and the shed door, it was not an accident. The shed door opened and my father fell to ground, the bull did not try to leave the barn, he just stood there looking at me. I know I was just a child and admittedly was afraid at that moment but I felt then and must confess I still do, the animal was well aware of what it had done. It showed no remorse. I was terrified by the beast and it knew I was but I had to shut the door. I walked slowly toward the shed and proceeded to close the door, I do not know where such composure had come from but I had use of it yet and prayed may it continue. What I had to do was transparently clear to me.

Father was a slight man, he had been a bulky, masculine figure in past years but did not eat much after mother died. Like the composure before, the strength came to me quite unexpectedly, from where I do not know. I carried him up to the ridge and buried him in the shade beside my mother, they had at last been reunited. The last words my father ever spoke to me were in his final seconds as he lay there on the ground and they were to tell me it was not his fault, meaning the bull. I left the bull well alone thereafter knowing better than to get too close. He was a bastard but I did not blame him for my father's death as was instructed.

I could not fight those men and felt hopeless, like I had felt hopeless when stood staring at the bull that day. I knew he could fight them all and had an idea he might, he never did take much in the way of provocation.

They rode up to the house at an easy pace laughing and celebrating, well that was their first mistake. This gave me time to think. I was terrified of them but the bull more so, again the strength and composure came to me. I waited for them to get closer and I ran to the bull shed, there were eight or nine of them couldn't be sure exactly how many. Just before I opened the door I looked back, three of them climbed down from their horses and ran after me toward the shed.

I made sure to be seen entering the shed and purposefully left the door open. My thoughts turned quickly from them to the bull as I entered, he was just standing there staring at me again. I looked him right in the eye but only for a moment. As I was only young and still small I climbed easily up one of the weight bearing supports up to the roof where I lay upon a timber cross beam and looked down. As the men entered the shed, 2 of them jested toward the bull, their second and final mistake.

I am not ashamed to openly admit that I gleefully anticipated the imminent result. He was a bastard but I was glad of that when he killed those men. One of whom was visibly ejected from the shed at a great pace, his body left the ground for a short while. He died where he landed and his body remained there to the best of knowledge, as did the bodies of the other men who died in the attack.The bull slowly wondered outside, it is my assumption that one of the remaining men shot at it, I heard a single gunshot before the bull charged off toward the direction where the men were. I heard many more gun shots to follow, amidst the noise the bull made and the gunfire I could hear the men shouting. I did not wait to find out what happened next. I climbed down the bearer to the ground and ran as fast as I could, I did not look back to see.

I did however recognize two of the men, just after mother died they came to the house to talk to father and though I did not know what about, I have a mind that it was about the house and the land. They seemed angry, it would not be honest to say that I was surprised they had come back. Wesley Morgan, one of two brothers who had made themselves outlaws many years ago when they raped and killed a whore over at the whorehouse. I confess I cannot understand the mind of an outlaw but I was confused and a little surprised they chose to do this in plain sight of everybody. Has been said that she offered to willingly participate but willing is not what they wanted, though I did not see Terry Morgan that does not mean that he was not there.

The second man I was able to identify was Fitzgerald, (Fitz) O'Hara, my father had previously described him as a greedy, ruthless son of a bitch but not a hard man to like. I guess Fitz and the Morgan brothers got the house and the land in the end, what became of the bull, I do not know.

    I left there and had no mind to go back, night fell on that day and I found myself in despair. I had previously thought myself so in the nights that I lay alone and cold in the dark back at the house. And again before that when I could hear my father downstairs sat by the fire, the cracking of the wood in the fire and squeaking of his wooden chair, mournful of my mother's passing. I was learning to re-evaluate my definition of despair, over and over again. By this point however I was quite sure that I had found the true definition of it, I was wrong again. I was afraid, cold, hungry and tired yet could not sleep. My attention was focused entirely on the howling in the distance, for reasons not known to me at the time I kept thinking about something my father had said just days before he died. He said, that which hurts us has a way of making us stronger. I took this to be true, he went on to say that only the strongest survive which I also believed to be true and still do.

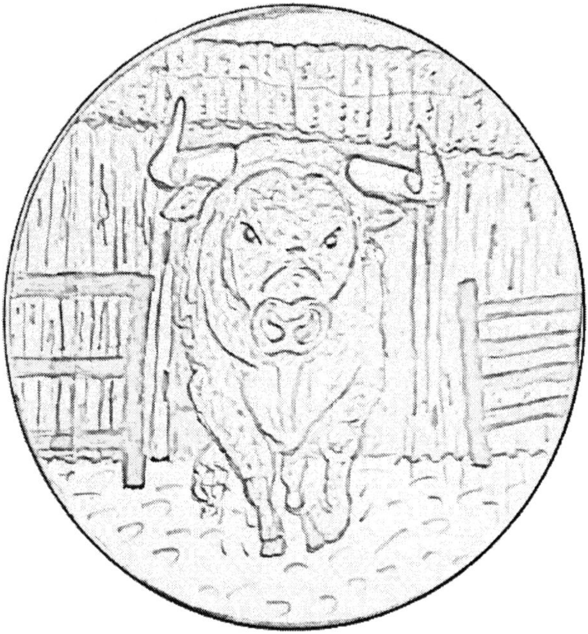

3RD.   GOING HOME.

As the sun rose the following morning I decided to go back, somehow I managed to survive till morning. I had reached the conclusion during the night that I would not last long out there under the stars without food, water, a gun, fire, blanket or horse. I had to accept my death either out there or at the house, didn't seem to matter much which. I recall seeing one of the men drop a pistol in the bull shed, it had fallen behind a bale of hay; I thought that it might still be there. When I got to the shed, stepping over the dead bodies, I looked behind the bale, the pistol was laying on the ground in front of me. I had seen my father thumb back the hammer and expose the barrel to count the bullets, I did as he had done so many times before using a pistol and checked the barrel to make sure it was loaded, I counted 2 bullets.

It was not a long walk back to the house but it seemed to take an eternity. I chose to go to the back of the house and climbed the side of the porch. I would have been seen from inside the house if I walked up the stairs. I was on the rear porch, on my knees under the bedroom window. I could hear the men talking but not in the bedroom, somewhere more distant.
I stood but I could only just reach the window, I could not open it all the way to the top and it would not stay halfway open. If it slammed shut I would be discovered. I reached inside and grabbed a stable hold then pulled myself up. I rested the weight of the window on my head as I climbed in, keeping the window open first with my head, then my back and finally let it down quietly with my foot.

    I stood in the bedroom with the gun in my hand, I could see through the gap of the open door, Fitz and two other men standing in the kitchen talking. Fitz was heading for the door, he left the house and walked across the yard to the outhouse. There were just two men left, I didn't recognize either of

them, it didn't matter I had 2 bullets. I
opened the door slowly then shot the man
closest to me, I missed the second. Like
many things in life, it did not turn out the
way I imagined. I had shot a man, an outlaw
but not killed or even seriously wounded
him. I shot his hand, as fate would have it
this would later lead to his death as it was
his gun hand.

Years later he would find himself in a
dispute at the saloon in town and not be able
to shoot his way out of it due to being the
only left handed gunman in town to carry a
right handed gun.

     After I shot the man it is fair to say
that I was to re-evaluate my definition of
despair once again. I had made a mistake
that would almost cost me my life, a mistake
that I had decided to never make again. I
can't say why but I did not try to run. The
man I had shot was closest to me, he struck
me so hard my ears were ringing. I fell to
the floor and by the time I tried to get up it
was too late, they were on top of me.

I had taken beatings before, I recall one such instance in town the summer before last.

My father and I went to the town. I had stolen alcohol from the store whilst father was talking to the store keeper, who was a son of a bitch and apparently thought nothing of beating a small boy. To this day I still wonder why my father did nothing, he just leant against the counter and watched. He looked me right in the eye and shook his head. At first I was angry with him. I think I understand now, some 10 seasons later. He was clearly disappointed and felt I should learn from this experience, I never stole again thereafter.

That day at the house as those two men were beating the hell out of me I recognized a face. Terry Morgan, the rapist. I guess I should not have been surprised when he started tearing of my clothes, apparently he saw no shame in the rough use of a boy only 10 - 12 years.

I had again been forced to re-evaluate my definition of despair. My left eye was starting to swell pretty bad by then and it was pretty much impossible to see anything out of it, I still had the ringing in my ears. When I saw Fitz walk in I was resolute my situation was about to worsen further, I have found that life is indeed full of surprises. The man whom I had shot seemed not to be interested in using me. He seemed more concerned with his hand, he had done the large share of the beating. Terry Morgan was the one who liked to forcibly insert his penis into folk whilst pinning them down.

    Fitz pulled Morgan off me, it is a shame he wasn't there a few minutes sooner. I think he was disgusted by Morgan. He inquired with the other man regarding his hand, then commanded that I be set loose. I had thought of it as a kindness at first, Fitz left the room and I heard the door to the front of the house close loudly. Morgan pulled up his pants and marched me to the kitchen door, I was ejected from the house with such force that I stumbled clear across the porch and down the stairs. I still couldn't see clearly but my hearing was starting to improve. I tried to run but was sore from both the beating and the sodomizing.

I wondered naked across my father's land up to the ridge where my parents had been buried, I felt in that moment that I would undoubtedly die and lay down to do so. Even though I wouldn't be buried here at least I would be close to them again and I warmed to the idea of dying and reuniting with them. That night I was so cold I couldn't feel anything, I had no idea a boy could be that cold and still survive.

Until that point I had 2 testicles, I will remember for the remainder of my life, however long that may be the night I lost track of one of them. At first I did not realize it but it had made its way into the body, it was so damn cold I couldn't feel anything else but the cold. Don't know where it went but I do get a kind of dull ache around the left hand side of my groin. It becomes painfull to touch.

I did not die and the following morning not long after I awoke; it was the first thing I noticed as I was trying to get warm in the light of the sun. I saw a glint of sunlight shimmering, moving in the distance then I realized it was a man riding up to the ridge, it was Morgan! I picked up a rock, the heaviest I could lift and hid behind the huge rock which cast shade over the graves of my mother and father. It occurred to me that he had followed a blood trail, then my assumption proved to be correct. He knelt down to dip 2 of his fingers in the blood I had left behind, where I had been laying.

    I called upon the strength and composure I had experienced before, this time it did not come. Instead I felt all consuming anger and my entire body was shaking with adrenalin.
I pulled out from behind the rock and struck Terry Morgan to the back of his head, he died where he fell. That was the first time I killed a man, there is nothing significant about that kill.
I have since killed many others and they all mean the same to me, nothing. I then stripped him and put on his clothes although they were way too big, it was my determination that it was better than being butt naked. I climbed on his horse and left,

it would be 3 winters before I went back to that house.

4TH. GROWING STRONGER.

    I had often heard men, a great deal of women too, curse the ageing of the body, mind and of years past and remark that they long for the restoration of their youth. I remained unconvinced and was prepared to trade my lingering youth for the growing of bones and muscles which would no doubt empower me to take all that the good people of Purgeatory had to threaten me with, not discounting the seasoning of the mind of course. I had no idea at that time just how much seasoning would be required, nor how much growing of the muscles and bones I was to be afforded, muscles in particular.

    Within 1 full season I had almost grown into Morgan's clothes, what a season it was. If hardship and endurance are the mandatory subjects of our education then I consider that season to be both my apprenticeship and qualification. Starvation and dehydration were pretty much a part of the daily routine living in the wild, I was untrusting of apparent opportunities after an incident during the first few days of being out there. I had come across a small pool of water, it wasn't clear like I expected water to be and had an aroma, as I recall it was almost completely still, I was put off by it but was so desperate for water. I knelt at the side of the water, cupped my hands and scooped some into my mouth, I had pretty much swallowed it as soon as it reached my dry throat.

Unfortunately that was also before I had tasted it. When I did taste it, I wished I hadn't. I lifted one of the large rocks on the surface to expose a larger surface I intended to take some more, in doing so exposed a lizard. The lizard jumped at me, I was on edge, a little bewildered and more asleep than awake. I fell backwards and without intending to I threw the rock I was holding at the lizard. I got up on my feet and continued about finding some water or food, within only a short time I felt as though there were one of those storms that go round in circles in my abdomen, shortly after that the nausea started. Can't say how long it lasted, the vomiting and the other problem continued day and night, I thought it might not ever stop. I was 10 or 12 then and I did not know what had happened to put my body into that state.

I realized years later when in conversation with another man at the saloon as he described the details of his son's death. He had known at the time that his son was dying of some disease or other caused by drinking stagnant water, which was a breeding ground for anything from animals to bacteria. He thought it was the bacteria that killed his son, I did not mention my experience at the time instead I sat and persisted with my attack on the bottle of bourbon I had purchased. I had a feeling of glee as I realized, I had survived that which had killed others the old man thought his son was 20 or so when he died, a much older man than me and would have been fully grown. I was proud that I had survived what a much older and stronger man did not. Whilst I celebrated, it occurred to me that I was accomplished at surviving.

That day was the first time I had that thought; it would become more familiar over the coming years. Although I did not know what it was, when the sickness finally left me I felt relieved. I had become frustrated with the consistency of anything and everything trying to kill me. I felt like it was personal, each time something or someone tried and failed I succumbed to celebration. I had even started taunting that which had offended me. It was like I had won a competition, I felt such highs after each battle even sometimes speaking aloud, "I survive again!"

A kind of legend had been growing in my head in the 2 full seasons that I spent wondering the wilderness, adding to it every time I triumphed over my attacker. I noticed a change in me at that time, in place of fear and despair I was feeling acceptance and determination. Instead of feeling sorry for myself for having to endure again, I was excited about another opportunity to win another battle and add to the legend.

The passing of that winter marked the end of that season and the beginning of a new year, somehow I knew that things would always be the same but I would be different. That boy was gone and it was gonna take more than an 1000lb bull to scare me, more than a disease from stagnant drinking water to kill me and finally, I would never allow someone to sodomize me again. I don't know what age I was at that point I guess somewhere between 11 & 13 I kind of lost track of the time. I knew that it had been at least a full season since my father died and I was forced to vacate the house.

    I was still wearing Morgan's clothes, they served as a reminder to me what people aim to do to me and will do if I don't stop them. It seemed like a different life when I put these clothes on and they hung off me. No such problem now in fact the trousers had become a little short in the leg although they fell off my waist and settled around the top of my legs. The shirt was tight across the chest and shoulders and a little short in the arms.

    The horse I took from Morgan run out on me just a few nights after I took it, I apparently failed to notice it had the ability to untie itself. I had to smile the following morning when I awoke as it reminded me of my father's horse, used to do that same trick my father did not see the funny side. Even to this day now as a man I cannot understand animals, the world of men I know only too well, it holds no surprises for me but when it comes to women and animals I am truly lost. One night as I lay there cold and wet looking up at the stars I come to the decision I was going to town, of course I knew it would not go over at all well but I was going. That is if I can remember the way.

  Last time I went with father was a long time ago, it was almost a full day's ride. We did it over 2 days but that was mostly due to the bull not being reasonable. If I could find my way I could probably do it in a day. I had pretty much run every place I went for the past year or so.
Looking back now I wish I had known which direction to head in, it was at least 3 days in the other direction. Shouldn't be a

problem except of course if I needed to get there quickly for some reason.

5ᵀᴴ.   TARANTULA.

I stopped to rest one night and I lay my head on a large rock it was almost perfectly smooth, it never occurred to me that I might be in danger. I was awoken at some point by a nuisance, well I must have raised my hand to my head to rid of whatever was bothering me. I felt something with the tips of my fingers and then again on my face, then a loud disturbance with my right ear. I woke suddenly and cast my eyes toward something close in the vision of my right eye it looked like a leg. It was a very small leg but being just in front of my right eye made it look like a very large leg. I knew what it was, damn thing caught me by surprise. I got up quick as I could and looked down on it, son bitch ran underneath the rock I put my head on, didn't occur to me to check under the rock. Just then I noticed a sort of stinging, first my right ear then again the fingertips of my right hand.

Son bitch stung me or bit me or whatever those things do! I was not impressed nor was I intimidated, would not be true to say I held no grudge. I picked up the rock and threw it behind me, damn thing ran so I ran after it. I suppose it would have been entertaining if there was anybody around to see it. I chased it for a short while then gave up. It ran under a rock I could not lift out of the way, then I noticed my whole face was stinging.

I touched my face with my right hand and it felt odd, didn't really feel like a face at all.

I looked down at my hand and my fingers were all fat and swollen. The same had happened to my face, it wasn't just swelling, it was damned irritating and kind of hurt. After I gave up chasing the spider I started walking, it was my intention to go into town, unfortunately I wasn't going anywhere for a while. I had taken a fever no doubt due to that damn bastard tarantula. I could see but my vision wasn't still, more like distorted. I felt cold even in the day time and I know how hot it gets this time of year in the day.

I wondered for a few days, how many exactly I don't know. I thought I was never gonna find my way, then quite unexpectedly a miracle happened. I had never actually ridden the train but I knew what it was, when I heard the unmistakable sound of the train's engine venting steam I was excited about the prospect of my first train ride. I thought I would run alongside the track and climb on the train, I missed the train by a long way, then fell on my face.
So I just walked the track believing it to lead into town, which it did eventually.

I finally got there but it took a whole bunch of nights, my face and hand were pretty much healed up by then and I think the fever had just about gone. I came into town on foot with no money and wearing a dead man's clothes. I am not surprised it did not go over well with the good folk of Purgeatory. Not entirely sure what I planned to do when I got there but it was fascinating. I listened to the people talking

and watched their face and body movements.
I guess I was studying them looking for pointers, trying to blend in was harder than I thought.

I will admit I am guilty of naivety, thinking that town would be a less harsh environment compared with the wilderness I had spent the last year or so. In many ways it was, but in others I dare say it was even more deadly. There was so much I did not understand about these people and about their ways but there had to be something else, some other reason for the way they looked at me. They could not have known at the time that I was unaccustomed to their ways, I know I didn't. I had not yet spoke with anyone, just my presence there seemed to be distracting.

I noticed something truly bewildering not just to me then but even to this day, the men and women seemed to flock in groups like the animals at the fair. I had only seen this strange behavior once before at the fair all those years past, the pigs all kept in 1 enclosure, the goats in another then the cattle and so on. All the animals segregated into smaller groups and then each group congregated together, then trapped. It is astonishing, all of gods animals mingling together, learning to tolerate one another and then somebody has the idea, segregate then congregate and then trap, it is quite beyond me. That said I was even more bewildered when I saw it in town and not among animals but people.

    I saw it first at the station segregated by sex, the women on one side of the platform and the men on the other, then again when I got to the center of town there was a group of five men outside the drug store they were all native. I saw another group outside the tailors, six women all white. Then again two black men walking on one side of the street and four white men walking in the same direction on the opposite side of the street, I was speechless. A few months later I discovered that there was only 2 places in town where all of the individual groups would co mingle, that was the saloon and the whorehouse. There seemed to be a kind of unspoken agreement or unwritten law, when it came to sex and alcohol all were alike.

6TH. GOING TO TOWN.

My presence was bothering just about everyone in town, though I was oblivious to it at the time I understand it now and can kind of picture it. A feral kid wearing a dead man's clothes walking around aimlessly staring at folk, with no money and no place to be.
I suppose it would be an accurate assessment to say that it was just a matter of time before somebody wanted to introduce me to their pistol, which of course happened eventually.

I did notice one thing that I was unable to explain although that is not unusual at all, my life was full of things that I couldn't explain. I didn't seem to fit any of the groups, I wasn't like the white men nor the native men. I was not like the black men or the latino men I seemed to not belong among any group. I continued my study of the herds roaming the town, their differences seemed to be of greater importance to them than their similarities. Some of the men seemed alike regardless of what group they belonged to but those men would not talk to each other.

There was a young man, native by the looks of him talking to young white lady outside the saloon. It was daytime and so the saloon was not open for custom although that did not stop people going in. I watched the young native man talking to his lady friend, I could hear most of what they were saying and I was not the only person who was watching. At least four groups stood outside various stores on both sides of the road. One group in particular, a small group of cowboys, four precisely, set out slowly walking toward the young couple in conversation. As my attention turned back to the couple she called the man charming, he smiled; I had to find out more about this charming thing.

He said she should have a chaperone on the account of this was no place for a beautiful young lady to walk around without a handsome and charming man to look out for her.

The strangest thing happened to that lady, her whole face seemed to change, she wore the prettiest smile I had seen and her face became a kind of pale reddish color. She tipped her head downward to the ground then raised her gaze upward back to the man and her eyes locked onto him. The most incredible eyes, I had never seen that before. It was as if there was a light radiating from behind her eyes or a fire. Each time she blinked, her eye lashes fluttered like butterflies. It was the most fetching display of feminine witchcraft. Truly you had to be there to properly appreciate it, I felt kind of strange almost weak or like I had been hypnotized.

That was the first time I had ever felt like that but I did not know at the time, I would get used to that feeling, real used to it. Just as I was stood there a helpless victim of witchcraft, mesmerized by this woman whom I would never meet.

The small group of slow moving cowboys had dramatically upped the pace and were on a path to the young couple. There were four of them as previously stated, well they attacked that young native man. She screamed and backed away, they knocked him to the ground and all four of them simultaneously proceeded to kick and stamp the young man. I truly had no idea what he had done wrong, 2 native men ran out of the saloon. I do mean the closed saloon and thank god because I was concerned that group were gonna kill that young man. There was a fight but it didn't last long, one of the men in group called one of the native men Wolf, many years later I learned that Wolf was somewhat of a leader to the native men and women in Purgeatory. The cowboy told Wolf that he would pay for this and that they would all pay for this. I had no idea what that meant but it seemed strange to me and that man seemed sick as if he had a madness. Wolf said nothing in response and just looked right at him.

After the group had gone Wolf spoke to the pretty young lady, he spoke politely and calmly but the message seemed clear even to me. He told her to be more careful,

he also said if she prayed to a spirit she should pray now for her spirits to protect her. She became tearful, as she wept she protested and in defense claimed she had nothing to do with it, those men were savages and she hated them all. Wolf put his hand on her right shoulder, looked into her eyes and smiled, he spoke again before he turned and walked away. "I know you were not responsible for those men, you have my word you have nothing to fear from me or my people."
I was talking about them.

    She ran off across the street, she was clearly inconsolable her tears soaking her lovely face. Wolf held out a hand to the young native man on the ground then pulled him up onto his feet, he warned him – "if you just got that young woman killed I will kill you myself." The young man bowed his head and seemed truly humble, not a display that I would observe in a white man until whole years passed. He spoke whilst looking toward the ground, sorry father my will was carried away on the wind and held prisoner behind her eyes. Wolf smiled turned and went back to the bar. The large mysterious man beside him watched Wolf go back into the saloon then he turned his attention to the young man, he spoke but I had never heard anything like his voice, was like thunder.

Dancing Moon, the young man lifted his head and looked toward the mysterious giant man. I took this to be a sure sign that Dancing Moon was the young man's name. Then the big man stepped forward, leant towards Dancing Moon and spoke again, I too was prisoner. He laughed loudly so much so that it echoed everywhere beneath the sky, he put his left arm across Dancing Moons shoulders and they walked into the saloon.

I learned a lot from this, one kind may not covet another and like bulls they kill their own kind as well as others. A wolf will come to fight for another wolf even if he thinks that other wolf is wrong. I was realizing how complicated the world of wolfs and men was, even if the old wolf saved the young wolf. If the young wolf was wrong the older and wiser wolf might still attack or even kill the young wolf depending on the severity of his offense. This was the way of the wolf and they believed in it, they all stood by this simple culture of simple laws and would protect their culture fiercely. I personally found this easy to understand and respected their commitment to it. I began to realize that a man's origin was the most important thing here and further more depending on your origin you might be looked after by your own kind, but each kind were different.

    The main differences I noticed were things like the relationship between the men and the women or the relationship between old men and young men. The native men didn't seem to be too kind toward their women and could be harsh toward their younger men and that seemed to be their way toward all of their own kind, harsh but fair regardless of whether it be man or woman, young or old. Seemed to be slightly different with the black community in town, they seemed to be much kinder to their young men, always supportive and constantly trying to inspire the young to be greater than they were.

There did appear to be a lot of fighting between the older men, they would fight amongst themselves and then put their differences aside so that they may be one united community.
Figuring that they were stronger together, until the next time they had to fight at least. The white community seemed at first to be the most divided. Many of the white men would not stand by their women on the train platform or sit at the same table in the saloon. It was as if they preferred the company of other men, in fact it was tough to tell who was in a relationship and who their alleged union was with.

Others among the men were openly affectionate and even compassionate toward their women and young, more so than the men in the other cultures in town. Interestingly these affectionate white men did not seem to mingle well with other men of any culture, just kind of kept themselves to themselves. The hardest group to figure out was the Latino community, partly due to the fact that there was not many in town and partly because they seemed to be the ones most intent to keep their feelings and intentions entirely to themselves. Although one thing remains true of all the people I had met in the town of Purgeatory and this the most important observation of all.

Whoever they were, men or women, young or old regardless of and including all of the various cultures in town, they were all different every single person was unique. Every person was individual even though their cultural divisions remained and they shared similarities with others of their own culture. Each culture seemed to have a wiser, older person who was trying to lead the rest to be more tolerant towards the other cultures; trying to keep the peace and in each culture that person was a man.

Among the natives that man was Wolf and his giant mysterious friend. In the black community that man was Ronnie, he had been a deputy and a champion sportsman, he too had a giant friend Sergeant Green who was a soldier in the American army and one of the people that I most looked up to. A couple of old cowboys Ed Henry and Harry Peters appeared to have the ear of the majority at least, of the white folk. The whole town seemed to either fear or respect Ed Henry and Harry Peters, they had been city marshals in Contention way back in the old days when it had been in their own words, a lawless hell hole. The Latino leader was a man simply known as Guerrero who was a living legend in Purgeatory and 3rd generation Guerrero to lead the Latino population of the town. In keeping with the tradition he too had a friend who was built more like a bull than a man and one of the strongest people I had ever seen, Hernandez. To me at least, they didn't seem to be that different all things considered.

7ᵀᴴ. DON'T BANK ON IT.

At some point I realized that I had what seemed to me a unique problem, incidentally I would go on to have more of those over the coming years. It seemed to me that I was the only person in the whole of Purgeatory who didn't have a culture, didn't belong to any group in particular. My father was a cowboy, a white man and my mother was not white. All the years growing up that the three of us used to go into town or go to the city fair it never occurred to me that we were different. Although in truth as I think back now we never really used to go anywhere that often, perhaps I have stumbled carelessly on the reason for that. My mother was native, she was a proud Apache woman, her religion and culture meant everything to her.

Honest as a rattle snakes intention to bite, it never occurred to me that they were different. They were just mother and father, ok they would fight like a rooster and a fox but I just assumed that was average behavior for a married couple. Though it would explain why I had to leave the first school when I was just a boy, it was a school for white boys. And also explain why I had to leave the second school too, since that was a native school.

I am half native and half white, 14 or 15 years, homeless, parentless wayward young man and this was apparently the first time this had occurred to me. Walking around town I guess I had accepted that I was never going to be like everyone else. I knew enough about myself to know that I would never be able to follow their rules or even learn them all, so I had to make the decision that I would not waste my time trying. Speaking of accepting things it had occurred to me that I may not have much of that anyway, time I mean.

I was unsure whether I was unlucky or luckier than I realized, I watched a small boy about the age I was when father died. My initial thought was that he was fortunate to have both a mother and father. Having spent a little time in town I was wondering if having family was really that great after all. After seeing the way they treat each other I mean, a boy wanted to go play with the other boys across the street, his mother was crystal clear when she forbid the very idea. Assumedly due to one simple fact, he was a white boy and the other boys were native, oh to see the world through the eyes of a child. The subject of all the excitement was a young lamb who had apparently gotten loose and now was running free in the street. Of course you can imagine that as far as a young boy was concerned this was a matter for further investigation.

So that boy ran across the street anyway and well you could be forgiven for thinking he had dynamite in his pockets. Talk about a stir, first the native adults stood on the sidewalk on the other side of the road started yelling and cursing. Then the boy's father ran across the street after him and when he caught up to him, gave that boy a hell of a slap. The boy's face took a color that I would say most resembles a tomato, and that boy cried out, sniveling and wailing being dragged literally across the street and I remember thinking how embarrassing.

In another example there was the young man who had finished school just days passed, he had gotten hired by the bank almost immediately after leaving school and had proposed to his sweetheart. I don't mind admitting I felt a certain degree of envy and did pray for his ruination, wish I had not. I came into town one morning just a few days later and well everybody in town was talking about it. Late in the night he had gotten arrested for some small misdemeanor and thrown in a jail cell for the night, the marshal could be heard saying, let him sleep it off. Whilst he was doing just that the 2 deputies who were supposed to be watching the jail cells, locked the whole place up and went to his house and helped themselves to his young fiancé.

That was the first time I had heard of the law enforcement behaving like the criminals they so openly despised, only a fool would think that would be the only time I encountered that.

I hung around for most of the day like most days just watching and listening. I had been coming into town daily for several weeks now then going back into the wilderness later in the day to find some food and rest.

A little later in the day that young man was released from the jail house, understandably the first thing he did was head off home to see his fiancé and presumably clean up. Within the space of a hour he found out that he had lost his job with the bank due to being locked up all night and that during the night 2 of Purgatory's finest law and order men helped themselves to his young wife to be who had been saving herself for their matrimonial night. Well anyway not too long after that he put his pistol to his head and killed himself, she eventually ended up working 6 nights a week at the whorehouse.

Life is a tragedy and that being said I'm not sure if the whole family thing is really for me after all. Least this way I could come and go as I please, do as I please and most of all I didn't have to worry about nobody else. I would not have to concern myself with whether or not my loved ones were ok seeing as there was no loved ones. I was always hearing how some man wanted to hurt or kill somebody else but didn't want to confront them in case he got shot. So they would just strike out at that person's loved ones instead. You could tell by the look on their faces they were all afraid to leave the house in case somebody broke in and killed their family while they were gone, which happened all the time. I was glad that there wasn't anybody to get hurt because of me or my actions.

    It meant that I was free to fight for myself without worrying about anything else other than winning this fight. I headed off into the wild that night with a spring in my step. I actually felt content with the way things were I had food when I need it, even if everything I ate made me sick. I didn't have a house to worry about, nobody could steal anything from me cause I didn't have anything worth taking. Didn't have a sweetheart to worry about or mother or father, even a dog. I was realizing just how free I really was, I liked it. I guess you could say my education was progressing nicely. Wasn't feeling sorry for myself anymore, even learnt to shoot and I had decided not to count on anything or anyone. I would plan 1 day at a time never looking any further forward than what I can see.

Take those men in town always saying things like "we will marry next spring" or "someday I will have my own house" or store or whatever it is that they wanted. Which did seem to me at that time and still does to this day little more than words without meanings. In my opinion if a man wants to wed his fiancé and she has no objection then you marry, right there and then, where ever you are. As for one day owning a store or a house well that at least I can understand, you can either afford it or not. I must assume that those who say one day, have not the necessary currency otherwise they would just go do it and stop talking about it.
In such cases I still believe that only a fool would put all his or her money in the bank, all in the name of days yet to come.

I am yet to see any such instance where both the money and person made it safely to that future day. That bank has been hit three times already this year and besides, the directors of the bank have apparently misplaced, mismanaged or misappropriated more money over the last 10 years than all of those bank robbers combined will ever see in a lifetime. There is also talk of a new public office coming to town which obviously will need to be funded by the good folk of Purgeatory. In addition to the already existing 4 public office buildings that currently are funded solely and completely by the public.

The town jail house including the city marshal's office and all of his deputies, then there's the courthouse, the office of city council governors and finally the bank. I knew instantly that whatever they promised I wanted nothing to do with any of it, the city marshal used to lock people up in the jail house for apparently no good reason and nobody was legally entitled to challenge him over this. The city marshal was the most corrupt individual in Purgeatory, his brother was one of the presiding members of the council of governors in the next town over.

As for the courthouse well I am not sure where to start, I can tell you that they heard over dozen cases while I was in town and it seemed to me that only the victims in the original altercations were guilty never the perpetrators. The office of city council governors, if you want to know what part in society they play then I would suggest you ask someone else because I have entirely no idea, I thought about it many times. I know for sure they find new ways to exploit the public to make more and more money for them to invest into hiring more deputies and expanding the capacity of the jail house so they can lock up more people.

From time to time somebody from the office of city council would go visit every business and home in town they would always be eloquent and polite but all the time processing information. They would only ever really ask questions but somehow you just immediately felt afraid to provide an answer. Any time you got a letter from the city council meant bad news especially if

it happened to coincide with a recent inspection, then it would be really bad news. There was kind of a pattern, whatever you said during the inspection would be in that letter, so if you were disgruntled and you said you were unhappy with amount of crime for example.
That letter would say something like.

During the visit a few key points were brought to our attention, as for the subject of crime within the city we want to reassure you that we are taking every necessary step to improve the situation, including introducing a new initiative to deter crime, however this initiative will come at a cost. We are pleased you have pledged your ongoing support and we want you to know that the increase in taxes you will pay will go toward funding this program. And then charge an extra 7 percent or something like that, if you said you were happy with the way things were then the letter might say something like. We are pleased that you recognize and appreciate our endeavors to make the town of Purgeatory a safer place, however this has come at a cost. We appreciate your ongoing support and we want you to know that the increase in taxes you will pay will go toward recovering the costs of these endeavors.

Basically you were screwed either way, the people they used for these inspections must have had what they call that photographic memory. I never seen any of them write notes or take photographs yet somehow they remembered everything. Any piece of furniture or clothing, even medicine, anything that was not there the previous visit their eyes would lock onto it as soon as they entered the room. You knew they were gonna ask when did you get that and how much was it. Any sign of something purchased since the last inspection meant somebody had more money than they were letting on, as sure as a wooden horse has a wooden dick you'd be getting a letter pretty soon.

There was only a few exceptions, the bank would be one of them; the bank was not subject to tax. The directors had a deal with the city council governors that if they were left alone then they would donate a large sum to the city council at the end of the year. That way the governors didn't pay tax on what they made from the bank and the bank didn't pay tax at all because they used money from folk's accounts to pay off the council. As I stated previously I am yet to hear of any instance where both the money and individual would be reunited all those years later.

    I can think of three such instances just whilst I been in town, a Mr Brownstone been saving every nickel he could. 25 years since he started putting his money in the bank and like most folk smart enough to know you gotta keep an up to date tally. He was smart enough to know he would need that tally one day to prove or disprove some kind of confrontation at the bank. Well word is he went in there a while back to claim his 100 dollars, a small fortune in the town of Purgeatory, he produced every receipt they had given him over the past 25 years.

He was eventually dragged out of there by two of the city marshal's deputies with 25 dollars and an order to not ever go back to the bank. 1 dollar per year he could have put that by in a jar in the kitchen, some men have put more than that behind the bar at the saloon or into the whorehouse. The bank had said that they were hit just a while back and that his was one of the accounts that had been taken and that he was lucky they were paying him the 25 dollars.

    In another altercation with the bank, Mr Macarthy was told that the bank had changed ownership within the last 10 years and any amounts of money he had in the bank previous the this current ownership was due to him by the previous ownership and not at all by any means the responsibility of this current group of directors. The only thing Mr Macarthy left with was a court order and 3 nights in the jailhouse which was the town's idea of a motel. It was all legitimate in the eyes of the law at least, they had written contracts for everything and all those ridiculous terms were hidden throughout the contract. I suppose that's the benefit of being among only a small number of people in the town who can read, so they hid these terms in the contracts and didn't never tell nobody about it. The moment that folk put their money in the bank, whether they knew it or not they had agreed to the terms of the contract.

How about this for curious and forgive my skepticism, when the news of Mr Gleeson's passing became public knowledge, the bank offered to close the account to the deceased's wife or son, knowing all too well that Mrs Gleeson was long since dead and Mr and Mrs Gleeson never had a son. They did have three daughters but coincidentally in the eyes of the law a daughter did not qualify. The most curious part of the whole thing is that on this occasion and I mean only this occasion, the bank offered to settle the full amount of that account, as I said forgive my skepticism. Obviously given that none of his daughters were able to claim it, the amount remained unclaimed and was reabsorbed back into the bank.

8TH. MIMI AND ME.

The next few years went by pretty fast, I got to know the law a whole lot better, in fact there are times I wonder maybe I have gotten to know the law a little too well. When I first started going to town I was pretty much left alone, didn't get in any trouble or even have anything to do with anybody else. Over a time things started to change, the first time I was dragged to the jail house I strongly protested, didn't do much good. At some point in the night, can't say when exactly, I was laid on a bed for the first time since my father died in a warm jail cell I had one thought, how long can I stay here. The following morning the deputy brought me some coffee, from that moment on I was hooked, on the coffee I mean not jail! Allthough I did end up spending a great amount of time there. He told me that I was released and not to come back, I almost cried.

For a lot of the young men in the town a night in the jail house meant being away from their own bed, away from whatever booze they were partial to and worst of all away from whatever means of obtaining a warm woman's body, for rather obvious reasons. For me however there was no downside to being in jail, due to the fact that I didn't have anything waiting for me on the outside. I got arrested and thrown in jail as often as I could during the winter at least as it was the only means I had of escaping the cold.

The court did fine me at one point, I didn't know what the hell a fine was. The judge explained to me that I would have to pay them money, I laughed for the first time in a whole lot of years. He said he would hold me in contempt, I got confused because I thought he meant Contention which was the next town over. He started getting angry, I didn't know what the hell was going on. He said I had to pay money so I told him I didn't never have any money a day in my life. In fact I wasn't really sure what money looked like, he asked me who my father was so I told him, he's dead. Then he asked about my mother, when I told him that she was dead too he sort of dropped his head, took a kind of long deep breath. He wanted to know all kinds of things like where I lived and what I did for food and if I had been to school.

He seemed to be getting more and more agitated until he asked me where I got the clothes that I was wearing, so I told him they belonged to Terry Morgan. Well I ain't never seen nothing like it, the whole courthouse seemed to erupt in a kind of frenzy the judge was hammering on his desk like a mad man. Everybody was shouting out and the judge was shouting out, it turned out to be the talk of the town for some time to come. Eventually it seemed to die down well in the courthouse at least, the judge asked me to explain that last remark and how I came by the clothes of a man who died around 5 years ago. I told him that I took the clothes from Morgan when I killed him because I was naked at the time and I was cold and couldn't go back to the house.

The judge's face pretty much changed color and he kept hammering on his desk, I'll be damned if I know what the whole hammer thing is all about. Then he had a whole bunch of other questions he said he wanted to go through it one at a time, first why did I kill Terry Morgan and how. So I said I killed him because he beat on me then he tore my clothes off, pinned me down and forced me. I ran out of the house and up on the ridge where my father was buried, he came after me and I hit him over the head with a rock.

Then he wanted to know what house, well as soon as I said 6 acre ranch, the whole thing blew up again. Some people had to be removed from the courthouse. Well the judge's hair was kind all over the place, his face was pale as a bed sheet, he did not look at all well. He had apparently worked out who my father was and subsequently who I was, he stated that I had been declared dead 5 years ago I had to laugh! He asked me to explain why I was laughing, I said it's because I ain't never been dead before, I didn't know what else to do. He ruled that Fitzgerald O'Hara and the Morgan boys had unlawfully taken the house and the land from me and that as far as the law was concerned Fitz had no legal claim to any of it and in the eyes of the law the land and everything on it belonged to me.

He insisted no further action be taken with regard to the death of Terry Morgan or any of the other men who died on the ranch that day, due to the fact that it was such a long time ago. There would be no evidence either way and Morgan was a convicted rapist and the judge saw no reason to question that the death of Morgan was indeed self-defense. He apologized to me that the law had failed to prevent O'Hara and his mob from forcing me out of my father's house and apologized to me that I had been abused by Morgan. He ordered that Fitzgerald O'Hara should vacate the land and be made to pay compensation, whatever that was. If he did not he would be arrested and held at the jail house.

As I was leaving the courthouse I was approached by 2 men. The first was Wolf, I was surprised he spoke to me, all he said was, now you're marked they will come for you.

I was just processing that and trying to figure out what it all meant and I was approached by another. Had no idea who he was at the time, I did find out later he was Morgan's cousin Wayne. I couldn't stand to talk to Wayne, he had the worst teeth I ever seen and the air between us had a kind of a stench when he spoke. He told me he would be coming for me, well that's exactly what Wolf said would happen. Like I said before I have taken some beatings but the one I was about to take kind of broke me a bit. I was on my way up to the ranch following the hearing, I was still a bit naïve about the ways of the world and the law. Whilst I was in town things were pretty frantic lots of people shouting.

As I got outside of the town limits it seemed to quiet down. I was aware that there were a lot of angry people, some of which seemed to direct their anger at me. I just somehow knew that I was being followed. It just occurred to me to turn round, I did not see who it was but I just about made out a figure of a man before I got hit in the face.

I'm not going to go into much detail here but I took a few hits, yeah I hit back too.
Got knocked down and honestly once I was on the ground any chance I had was pretty much over, I made out four of them. I got a couple of kicks to the body but it was mostly headshots, I felt my nose break first, that was pretty early on. My eyes started to close up next then I got kicked round about the ribs and as soon as it landed I knew something broke. I started spitting up blood soon after, son bitch kicked like a mule. One of them stamped down on my genitals that hurt, it didn't seem to go on that long when they had enough they stepped back. I thought it was pretty much over. The skinny one had a knife 2 other men held me down then that skinny old bastard cut me, I still got the scar.

He turned the knife around and stabbed me right in the damn chest! What a son of a bitch, I was powerless against them this time and had to just suck it up. I knew that I would survive and that one day the careless son of a bitch would be out here by himself and I was gonna kill him with his own knife, not doubt about it. They left me there I guess they thought they did a good enough job I would just lay there and die, not on your life. If they thought that would kill me then they just don't know me at all. Yeah I laid there for a while caught my breath, started feeling cold and weak and I had lost a lot of blood. I got up and stumbled slowly back to town. I wasn't far outside of the town. Holding my chest with my fingers pretty much covered in blood, I found my way back into the edge of town right near to the whorehouse. I fell down to the floor with a thud.

      Someone was walking by as I passed out!

A pretty girl took me in, she had a room at the whorehouse. She had as far as I can see no reason at all but she cared for me and cleaned up all the blood. I rested up for a few days she fed me and gave me some liquor, I think it was supposed to be for the wound. I didn't know how to thank her. The whole looking out for me thing was new to me, she just smiled and pointed out that she was a whore. I mean there would be plenty of opportunity for me to return the favor in fact she expected that any day now some no good bastard would try to beat the hell out of her. I had been fighting all of my life and never really knew what I was fighting for. I kind of liked the idea that I would be fighting for something, for someone.

    I was concerned that I would fall for this girl, in truth I already had. I mean it didn't take a lot, just to stitch up the hole that knife had made in my body, wash the blood of me and provide me with bourbon. Hell, I was head over heels. That would be fine if she had absolutely no interest in me, so I had to find out was there any interest. She was pretty cool about it and once again reminded me that she was a whore. Meaning that love wasn't really a subject she thought about but went on to reassure me, don't worry I am not going to fall in love with you.

The fact that it was an insult made it easier to believe she spoke the truth and the fact that it was a reassurance made it easier to take the insult. She owed a small bill at the haberdashery because of me and the chicken and bourbon would not have been free. Worst part is she remarked on how she, "lost 2 days' work" on the account of having a bloody young man in her bed.

    Well I felt bad enough but when I asked her where she slept and she told me she spent the past 2 nights in the chair I was mortified. I was angry at myself and decided next time it happened I was not gonna turn heel and crawl into town like a rat, end up costing some poor girl. I was not gonna put on anyone ever again, I never wanted to feel this again, I felt such shame. Next time I'm bleeding to death out there in the wild like a man, to hell with this being somebodies charity case. I now had 2 feelings, the first is that I so wanted to get close to her. Just to touch her, hold her and spend the night with her.

    That wasn't gonna be easy, the second thing was that I didn't have any means of paying her back, I had nothing to offer her. The only thing I could think of was that she must hate living here at the whorehouse and if she had a chance she would leave in a split second and would be delighted by the prospect of having free run of 6 acre ranch. I told her about it and made sure to point out that she wouldn't owe me anything, I wouldn't expect her to share my bed even though secretly I was hoping for it. I thought she would jump at the offer but instead she turned me down, I didn't get it, still don't. Anyway she wouldn't go for it and wasn't falling for the not expecting you to share my bed thing, she saw straight through that. Wouldn't lay down with me. Seemed repulsed by the idea of me paying for her services. She had no idea how much she hurt me, I left there as quick as I could. I never felt so terrible in my life and it was all I could think about.

    It just kept going over and over in my head. I wish I had stayed out there laying down in the dirt, I wish I had died out there like a man. She didn't want anything from me, she didn't even want the money for the haberdashers. If she hated me so much then why did she do all that she had done for me. Either way I had learnt a new respect for the girls that live and work here. Most people just saw a whore which they felt they could do with whatever they wanted and mostly that's what they did. I didn't like it I saw something different when I looked at Mimi, she was a person, a kind and attractive woman, smart too. More than that she was brave and strong and she just did what she had to do even though she hated it.

9 TH. WAYNE MORGAN.

I had been wounded by Mimi and she would not accept any help from me in return and I couldn't shake that useless unwanted feeling so I decided to do something about it. Thinking back to a conversation with Sgt Green, well not really a conversation more of a passing comment, I was just drawn to the guy and wanted to talk to him. He obviously didn't want to be bothered by some kid besides there was clearly pressure on each of the cultural groups not to mingle with others outside their own culture. Respectfully, I didn't give a damn about that, I wanted to talk to him. He did eventually give in and exchange words with me. "Why do you keep bothering me??" He kind of barked at me, I just wanted to talk to the man so that's what I said, I wasn't surprised when he asked me why. Wasn't really sure what to say so just tried to be honest, never met a soldier before I guess I was kind of impressed by the uniform and the way he wore it. A soldier wears many different clothes but the way a soldier wears his uniform is entirely different to the way that he wears anything else.

When he asked me if I was impressed by the soldier uniform I stopped trying to be honest and went with the obvious. I think he saw right through it, he smiled. He did suggest that if it was something that I was interested in which I clearly was then I should go sign up. He said it would make a man of me and give me the chance to find myself. He also said that after I served my country, I would have earned my place and that most importantly I would gain all the skills a young man needed to survive in this chaos. I had decided that was how I would grow into the man I wanted to be, tough and smart and had something to offer a woman. I was going and there was not a damn thing that would ever stop me.

I didn't realize how much time had passed, like I said before I lost track of time and in truth this happened regularly. It had been 5 years since that day up at the house and things sure had changed in that time. I had been coming into town pretty much daily for that whole time. I felt like I had learnt a lot about Purgeatory and grown a lot as a person. It was my intention to sign up with the army but I would have to wait a while. They would be coming back to Purgeatory the coming spring and I could sign up then. It was summer at the time so I guess I had almost a year.

    I tried to see Mimi but I couldn't get near her the whorehouse didn't have many rules but they had one which would not be open to debate. No money, no honey and I guess by honey they meant sex. I wanted to just try to tie up some loose ends before the spring. I kind of knew Fitz wasn't just gonna give the house up because a judge said he should. I still wanted to get closer to Mimi and was waiting for somebody to try and rough her up so I would have a chance to repay her. I needed to find some kind of work before I left for the military so that I could pay back what I owed to Mimi even though she insisted I didn't. I was in town trying to find some kind of work, I was asking around but nobody really wanted to talk to me.

You remember Dancing Moon, he was the young native man who got in trouble a while back for talking to that pretty white girl. A few days later they were seen kissing by 2 men, probably those cowboys. Dancing Moon got the hell beat out of him and then they turned on the girl, beat her face pretty good then pinned her down and forced her. That time there was no-one around to stop them. They were both forbidden to ever see each other again and last I heard they were each fully recovered from their ordeal. But this is Purgeatory and that wouldn't be the end of it. There was a poster outside the courthouse and then again outside the jail house, wanted and then the profiles of 2 men. I recognized that dirty son bitch Wayne and the other no good bastard, the skinny old man with the knife. They were obviously an effective group but I was willing to bet that one on one they wouldn't take much before they were begging for mercy. I knew what I was going to do but I just wanted to speak with the girl first.

Issobella seemed to be just about the only young woman in Purgeatory who wasn't working at the whorehouse. I saw her in the street with her father. I approached cautiously, her father wasn't none too pleased about it but I somehow managed to convince them both to at least hear me out. I told her that I knew who those men were and that I knew what they had done to her. Before she became too sorrowful I tried to get to the point, I told her what they did to me. When I said what I intended to do and asked her how she felt about that her face lit up and I do believe that was the first smile in a long time. I hated seeing her walking around the place looking like the living dead. The smile on her face used to light up the whole town now she looked like she may never be happy again. I was starting to get used to this among the many young women in this town. That is what this place does, it eats people and strips them of all which made them who they were. I was thinking about doing things my own way, starting with Wayne and that other son of a bitch.

I knew that I would find them sooner or later and I was positively energized when I saw that skinny old bastard stood out the back of the saloon urinating. All his friends were inside the noisy saloon drinking and having a good time. Shame, it meant that they wouldn't be able to hear him cry out for help. I felt like I had to prove myself and this was it, it starts now.

I quietly crept up behind him and just kind of stood there. I hadn't ever done anything like this before, wasn't sure what to do. As I stood there I looked down and saw his blade tucked into his boot. That is the knife he stabbed me with, what happened next is the first time I really found out who I was. My hands were shaking and as I looked down at that blade I seemed to kind of lose track of everything else. I was entirely focused on him and me and nothing else entered my head. I had never experienced such single mindedness or clear head, it was as if there was no outside world nothing else other than the 2 of us.

As I took his knife he turned round and looked right at me, didn't say anything just stood there. I had no mind to do anything other than beat him, I got off several good hits and he kept hitting me back. I was surprised by how well he was taking the hits and dare say he was also surprised by me and how well I was. I did eventually get the better of him, I knew I would. He was getting tired and couldn't keep it up for long, where as I could do this all day and this time I was buzzing with so much adrenalin that I couldn't even fell my face or hands. I got him down and just kept striking him with my fists in a downward motion, it was a bit like that judge hammering on his desk. I kept hammering on his face and head and then I stopped and I could barely stand, my legs felt so weak. My hands were still shaking and now my arms felt so heavy I could barely lift them. I took his right hand, held it against the outside of the saloon and put his knife through his hand into the wood. Then I stumbled away, made my way outside town limits back to where I had been staying.

I did not sleep a bit that night and knew there would be consequences, I was confused about who I was. I didn't want to become him or be anything like any of those men but I didn't want to be like that poor girl either. Out here, there was no law against beating someone or killing someone just so long as you had a good reason. If you didn't then you might have to face the judge or the city marshal but mostly you'd probly get away with it. As far as the law goes at least, although there would almost certainly be a retaliation from the locals, whomever was affiliated with the victim.

The next time I went to town I saw Issobella, she positively ran to me and put her arms around me. That was the first hug I ever had, by god I nearly fainted. Was just about trying to cope with that then she kissed me! Ok, it was only a quick kiss but that doesn't change anything. There was kind of an energy coursing through my entire body, I don't know what that was. She thanked me then smiled, the whole way across her face her eyes lit up like the stars in the sky. She turned and then glided across the street. I couldn't stop thinking about it, the way she smelt. Her soft, warm, slight body held against mine, the softness of her lips against mine. I completely forgot about Wayne or the man I nearly beat to death, I completely forgot about everything. Good and bad came from my actions, the good was that Mimi had heard about what happened and seemed to be have warmed to the idea that I might one day fight for her like I did Issobella.

Wolf and Dancing Moon approached me in the street, I thought I was gonna be beat to death on the account of being kissed by Dancing Moon's love interest. Wolf just kind of stood back, I think he was keeping look out. Dancing Moon spoke to me quite unexpectedly, he issued me with a promise. Natives were pack animals, just like wolves. He said that if I came to his aid when he called then he would come to mine when I called. Wolf then went on to issue a warning about standing up for myself and that lone wolves don't last long. Seeing as I was not a pack animal and there was no herd who would ever let me be part of it I had to accept that it would not be a long life. I do wish that Wolf, as wise as he is, would stop making predictions with regards to my life because so far every time he says something is going to happen, it does.

Yeah Wayne and the remaining 2 of his group were waiting for me at the town limits. I wish I had the sense to avoid disputes like that. I guess some men have both balls and brains, I seemed to be desperately lacking one of those. Thankfully they made it easy for me, Wayne and his buddy Spit stayed back and sent the other one to come get me. He started walking toward me, I could see clearly he raised his pistol, son bitch shot me right in the leg. I was thinking about what Wolf said about lone wolves.

As I laid there I decided to play dead and listened to the footsteps in the dirt. My plan was to wait till he got closer then surprise him, I grabbed a good handful of dirt and stared straight up to the sky then he entered my vision. Just as soon as he got to me he raised his pistol again, I think I had horribly misjudged the situation, I had a habit of doing that. Well it occurred to me that if I was gonna act I had better do it quick cause he was about to shoot me again. I threw the dirt right in his face and got up as quick as possible, he shot again but thankfully missed me that time. He was waving the gun around like a crazy person just firing at anything even though he couldn't see what he was shooting at. I ran round behind him and bent down to pick up a rock, I was just watching the pistol and making sure wherever it was pointing is where I was not standing. Both Wayne and Spit were running towards me then the most unlikely thing happened, as I bent down to pick up the rock Wayne shot at me, missed me and hit his own man. I just about realized what happened, just stood there looking down at the gun in the dead guys hand, the other two fired a few more times, one of which almost hit me.

    I dropped the rock, fell on the dead guy and picked up his gun. I pointed it toward Wayne and squeezed the trigger. I missed the first time and thank god I hit him the second time, the gun was empty. I just dropped it and ran behind the bush. My hands were shaking again and I felt like I wanted to attack them, couldn't even feel the bullet in my leg. It was like before outside the saloon, one single vision. I was set on hunting them two men and by god I was gonna get 'em, whatever the cost. Wayne was down but he was alive, Spit tried to check on him but he didn't want that, he sent Spit on after me. I stayed behind the bush and could see through it quite well. He was walking towards me firing his pistol, 2 things were clear the first being that he was a lousy shot and the other that he would soon be out of bullets if he kept this up. Then just like that he was out of bullets, as he got closer I ambushed him, I had a smaller rock in my right hand.

    I dove out from behind the bush and struck him with the rock in my hand. Wayne kept shooting and I had a mind that, seeing as he had already shot one of his men, he might just shoot the other. I hit him again just to make sure and he seemed pretty out of it, I held his body up in front of mine and walked it back toward Wayne. He kept

squeezing the trigger and hit Spit a couple of times, when he stopped firing I came to the conclusion that he was out of bullets. I dropped the body and ran after him, he made it to his feet and seemed ready for me.
We exchanged blows for a while but I had that single mindedness again, like I had been set on a course and that was it, nothing could divert me. I eventually won out and got him down, I know his pistol was out of bullets but I have been hit with the butt of a pistol and I know it hurts and whole bunch more than a fist. I just kept striking him with the pistol to the head, he passed out I think, I hit him a couple more times then passed out on the ground.

    When I awoke the next morning. I can't say I was surprised but I was a little relieved. I awoke to three dead men, and a bloody hole in my leg which was attracting flies and ants. I'll be damned if I going to be anybody's charity case again, so I was gonna go into town and just carry on as normal and I suspected that I would be thrown in jail and put up in front of the judge again. Well you will no doubt be unsurprised to find out that's exactly what happened.

10TH. GET A ROOM.

While I was awaiting verdict over the incident a few nights back the marshal had a native woman come in and clean up my leg, apparently it had gotten infected. I had lots of visitors which was a shock to me, and every morning the deputy brought me coffee. Mimi came to see me and wanted to know what happened and why I did it that was the standard set of questions for all the visitors. Issobella and even SGT Green asked the same set of questions. Issobella came to see if I was ok. Dancing Moon came up to the jail house but they wouldn't let him in what with him being native and all.

Two of the deputies had family ties to the old man who cut me up. Turns out he was Roland Barnaby, cousin of Jake Barnaby who used to be a deputy here. He died in a shootout that was a long time ago but the two deputies who like to come into my cell each night and try to beat the hell out of me were Jake Barnaby's sons. I didn't catch their names, this of course is because it wasn't important to me what name they went by. I didn't have long now till the spring when I could sign up for the army. That is of course if I'm not still locked up in here and if I'm still alive. I didn't mind too much the Barnaby's coming in here each night, I felt like it kept me sharp. My face swelled up at the beginning of the week and just kind of stayed that way the whole week.

    I had been notified that I would see the judge Saturday morning and was facing 3 counts of murder. The marshal said that there would be a lawyer at the court who would help me, if I wanted he could arrange for the lawyer to come here and talk to me before Saturday. I was just waiting for the lawyer to call by, dealing with the two Barnaby idiot's and just sort of relaxing a while. Had nothing to do and no place to be and for a while at least it was refreshing to have the change.

The last time Mimi came to see me I was distracted the whole time by the deputy on duty at the time, I had noticed that some of them were just ordinary men, decent men. Others were murdering, rapist criminals in uniform, and I guess that is in keeping with the rest of my findings so far. Whether it be lawmen, judges, cowboys or whores there was good ones and bad ones in all kinds. Anyway I saw the deputy looking at Mimi and I. It wasn't just that he was looking that worried me, it was the way he was looking at her, I had to interrupt her and told her to leave. I could see she was offended by this and tried to find a way to explain without giving too much away. I told her that the deputies had been asking questions about her visits and what the relationship was between us. I just tried to be honest about it, said that I was concerned he would do something horrible if she kept coming to see me. She seemed upset but I think she understood what I was trying to say, she promised not to come see me again.

Later that day I was just about to fall asleep in my cell and I heard a disturbance outside the jail house. I was desperately trying to see outside to see what it was but I couldn't see outside from my cell as it was on the wrong side of the jail house. It was about an hour or so after that son bitch deputy Webster had finished his shift, the guy who had replaced him was to my mind one of the good ones, Eddie Sanchez. He went to take a look outside, I asked him what he saw but he was reluctant to tell me anything. I had a suspicion and it was getting worse, I called him over to my cell and I asked him to do something. This of course was highly irregular for a prisoner to make requests but I knew how seriously Eddie took the law and I had a mind that he might be interested, if he was then he might just save somebody. He looked at me square ways for a moment before asking me what I was thinking. I asked him about when he looked outside to see what the disturbance was, "did it have anything to do with the whorehouse?" He just looked at me, wasn't saying anything either way.

    I took that to be a confirmation, now I was sure not suspicious anymore and was getting desperate to do something about it. I spilled the whole thing I don't think he was buying it. I told him look at the facts, Webster was in here earlier giving her dirty looks. He stared at her for about 10 minutes straight, then just after he got off work there's a stir at the whorehouse. Come on don't ignore this, you got to do something before someone gets hurt. He was thinking about it then he asked me "if there is something going on up there then how come nobody has called?"

    I was gonna have to be careful how I put the next line together, "if I'm right there's a deputy working over a whore up at the whorehouse, who's gonna call!" Just like that his face changed shape he picked up the telephone and called the whorehouse. He asked if everything was ok there. The proprietor was not a silly man he would have to be careful what he said but he did care for the girls. I have no idea what he said but whatever it was Eddie didn't like it none too much, he just said "I'll be right there" then hung the phone up He grabbed the keys to the jail house and ran out, he was in such a hurry he didn't lock up the jail properly. While he was gone I was pacing my cell like a wild animal, I just wanted to get out. It was driving me crazy that Mimi was likely being attacked and I couldn't get there to help her, worse still that it was because of me. Then to my surprise the jail house door opened and I could see somebody coming in, I was relieved when I could see it was Dancing Moon.

He came to my cell and told what I least wanted to hear, it was a disturbance up at the whorehouse, I know it was Mimi. I asked him if he meant what he said before about coming to my aid when I called and vice versa, he was cool about it and just said "what do you want me to do?" I asked him to get up there and do whatever he could for Mimi, I was building a respect for Moon. He just dipped his head and ran for the door then it occurred to me that Issobella had been coming to see me too, she might be in trouble. Then it occurred to me that Moon would do just about anything for Issobella, I wanted to mention it but would have to do so before it was too late and Moon was off out the door.

I yelled out "wait…!" He stopped just outside the door and turned, so I cut to the punch line, "Issobella she…" and before I had a chance to finish saying what I was trying to say he interrupted me and said, "I know." I tried to clear it up for Issobella's sake and went on the defensive, "there is nothing…" then again he interrupted and again just said "I know."
I got to the point, "she might be..." He just smiled at me and said "I know", after that he turned and ran out.

Not long after Eddie came back and when he got to the door he realized he hadn't locked it when he left. He asked me, "anybody been by whilst I was away?" Before I answered I looked at the old man in the cell across from me, he smiled at me then laid down and pulled his hat over his face. I looked to the right there was one more in the cell next to me but he was out cold, had been all night and stank of alcohol. I looked at Eddie and said "no one had been up here, what did he find? What was going on at the whorehouse? " He was clearly frustrated and pointed out that I was a prisoner awaiting trial he should not be talking to me, besides he didn't have to provide me with any answers. I respected that and knew it to be true but I had to know, "just tell me this, is she ok?" He just said, "She'll be fine", I knew that was the end of the conversation, just 2 more days then I will know whether I'm getting out of here or not, Saturday morning couldn't come quick enough.

    Saturday morning came and I just wanted to get it over with. The marshal himself walked me to the courthouse, it was packed again. I was a little relieved to have the same judge as the last time I was here. Had that same look on his face as before agitated, unimpressed as if he was being pulled away from some important thing he had going on elsewhere. I spoke to the lawyer late Friday afternoon with regards to the charges I would face, he said 3 counts of premeditated murder, if found guilty I might hang. I said more like 1 count of murder in self-defense, he said I still might hang I wasn't holding onto high expectations for my freedom or future. We agreed on how I was gonna plead and what explanation I would give to support my claim, so I told him exactly what happened.

Well when I got to the courthouse I couldn't see him anywhere. I asked one of the court employees if they knew where Mr Pennyworth was, I was kind of confused when they told me he hadn't been there at all that day. It had never occurred to me that he might not show, might not do anything to represent me at all. Well, he never did show so I took on the job myself just like last time and just like last time I decided I wasn't gonna try to be smart. Just tell the truth and let the court come to whatever decision.

He got right down to business, the first words he spoke were to read out the charges against me, you are accused of 3 counts of murder premeditated, all by way of shooting, if the court finds you guilty today you will be sentenced to 5 years as a prisoner in the main city jail in Silver City. How do you plead? As if I was ever gonna say I did it, I'm no expert so I hope the court forgave me if I didn't say it exactly right but I just said what I told the lawyer, "1 account sir. Wayne Morgan and the gunshot didn't kill him, I beat him to death with the butt of his pistol, the other two were shot by Wayne himself." There was a lawyer there but he was clearly not there to speak on my behalf, more like he was trying to tie a noose around my neck. Soon as I made my opening statement he stood up screaming at me, telling the judge and everybody else in the courthouse that I was a damned liar, he said that was all lies.

    The judge asked him not to interrupt and told him that he would have his time to speak then told him sit down. He then came back to me and asked me if I expected him to believe that? I wasn't really sure what he meant, "yes sir I do." Then there was a lot of gasping and whispering around the court, I'll be honest I didn't really understand the whole trial thing but I wanted to pretend I did, I figured if they found out I didn't understand they would use it against me. When he said he didn't, I didn't know what I was supposed to say so I just stuck to the truth, "I'm sorry you don't believe it sir but whether you believe it or not that is what happened." I didn't know if he was gonna be upset by what I said or not but he was relaxed about it, Mr Whyte thinks you are lying about the events that took place, what do you say to him? Again I was in over my head, "well sir I'm not lying, what I said happened is exactly what happened." The judge pointed out that Mr Whyte says otherwise, so I pointed out that Mr Whyte wasn't there, therefore how can he honestly have any idea what happened? I mean it's not like there was anybody else there who saw what happened and could have told him.

    He considered what I said then spoke a little with Mr Whyte, "well Mr Whyte, the defendant says you were not there, what do you say to that?" Well what could he say? Then the judge asked him, "the defendant points out that considering you were not there, and there was nobody else present who could have given you a firsthand testimony of what happened you have no way of knowing", so again he agreed. "Then how can you be sure that what the defendant is claiming is a lie?" I would say Mr Whyte looked uncomfortable, he spent a lot of time fanning his face with the report in his hand. I was asked if I could provide any proof of what I say happened. I wasn't really sure what proof was, I think I made the mistake of misunderstanding him. I just walked him through step by step what happened, starting with the old bastard outside the saloon up to the point that I passed out.

    I remember something my mother told me when I was just a boy.
She was asking if I had helped myself to the jug of water she had placed on the table, I had, but went with the lie. She had a way of explaining things that I had not found in anybody else. She told me that however good a lie, it's still a lie and only the truth will ever sound anything like the truth. Of course that made no sense to me at the time and I had no idea what it meant but standing there in front of the judge, I think I finally understood it. I figured he would know the difference, would know the truth when he heard it.

It all sounds plausible young man but I asked you for proof, which you still haven't given me. I felt like an idiot and didn't want to ask but I had no choice, "what do you mean by proof sir?" It was against the rules of the court for a defendant to press the judge to form his defense, but due to the fact that I had clearly no idea about any of these legal proceedings and due to my lawyer not turning up, I guess he felt compelled to play along. He asked one question at a time, then asked me to give evidence that would convince the court that it happened the way I say and could not have happened any other way.

    I just answered his questions honestly and as clearly as I could being sure to point out things like; I never owned a gun and they were gunmen. Why would anybody believe that I, unarmed and alone would pick a gunfight with three known gunmen? That seemed to be a small success, I was also keen to point out that two men were shot on the ridge that looks down on the town, Wayne was shot further away where the horses were tied. How could I have been standing where Wayne was when I shot the other two men and standing where they were when I shot Wayne? They would have had my head long before then. What was nice is that by this point Mr Whyte had stopped shouting at me and calling me a liar.

I came to the assumption that there is no way, no progression of unlikely events that would allow me unarmed, to walk up to the ridge where three armed dangerous gunmen were not waiting for somebody, disarm one of them, shoot him, then shoot myself. Then walk over to Spit and Wayne who was no fool, shoot Wayne, disarm him then using his pistol shoot Spit twice who would have been running away from me at the time due to the positioning of his body. Then turn my attention back to Wayne and beat him to death with the butt of his own gun and after all that, live to tell the tale. I think that must have pretty much done it because Mr Whyte looked very disappointed and kind of slumped into his chair, he put his pen down and closed the file on the table in front of him.

I did feel bad for the judge though, I had been in front of him a whole bunch of times and he seemed to dread hearing my cases. I didn't dread being up in front of him like most did in fact I liked him and quite enjoyed our conversations. I used to always smile when I was dragged into the room, I'd look right at him and say hello! He would kind of look at me like 'dear god not him again.' On this occasion he was forced to accept that I was indeed set upon by those three men. That they were indeed waiting for me at the town limits that I was indeed defending myself. He was forced to lower the charges from 3 counts of premeditated murder to 1 count of murder in self-defense and added one count of battery with intention for Barnaby. I got 1 year in city jail in Silver City.

Then I asked if there would be any chance that I would be free to join the army in the spring when they came back round since I had been waiting till I was old enough to join and would be 16 when they returned the coming spring. He closed his eyes and took a long breath, I had upset him again but I wasn't doing it intentionally. I didn't know what I said wrong, he leant back in his chair and looked up to the ceiling. "how old are you young man?" I said, "15 sir, I think." He then changed his verdict, on the account of a man had to at least 16 to go to the main city jail in Silver City, just like the army. He didn't realize I wasn't 16 yet and the law would not permit the incarceration of a 15 year old in a city jail, so I would be held in Purgeatory. He also stated that my intention to join the army would reduce my sentence due to the fact that it was serving my country. So when the army came I would most certainly be released to the army. So all things considered it didn't turn out so bad.

11TH. JUDGE WOODROOF.

Judge Woodroof was a decent and fair man, he could be hard but there is nothing out here that is not. It was understood that his primary concern in all cases was the integrity of the law and felt like it had become threatened in these modern times as the world continued to change, with the development of technologies and people having more choices than ever, somehow the law would get left behind. The previous judge had been the unexpected benefactor of a large amount of money right before a trial, which seemed to just about everybody in the city except him to be crystal clear.

There had been a boy 16 - 17 He was an African American boy, he had a sweetheart who was an African American girl around the same age. In a turn of events typical of the good 'ol town of Purgeatory. They had been attacked by a group of good old boys. As far as I can tell the reason for this attack was nothing other than that young couple were too dark for the group's liking. Anyway she had become upset and tried to make a run for it, fearing that she might get help, one of the cowboys shot her down. The young man heartbroken as any man would be did his very best to try fight off his attackers. Unfortunately he was outmatched and they beat him to death.

When it came to the trial, the judge had one witness statement and a whole bunch of other evidence to draw on in order to reach the correct conclusion. He somehow failed to do so and judged that the young black man had seen the four good old boys and had the idea that he would try to prove himself to his young sweetheart by assaulting them. It had backfired on him and he was killed in self-defense, she was accidentally killed by a stray bullet carelessly set loose by the young man when he reached for the cowboy's gun. There was an uprising, quite understandably and at first it started out as being directed at the judge, which was correct.

That went over like shit on a biscuit so in a master stroke only the law would be capable of, the anger at this miscarriage of justice got somehow redirected at the Irish American community. So that instead of the people fighting against the corruption of the law, they torn each other to pieces in the streets. It was Wolf who tried to mediate and pointed out that war between the people was the wrong fight, a joint war against the corruption was the right one.

Which is correct on all counts. He should know given the amount of experience he has had with those kind of situations, it happens all the time in Purgeatory more so to the natives.

His own daughter was lost, that would have to be 20 years ago now. Well after that he was at war with everyone and everything, nobody ever told him what happened or who done it all he knew about it was he and Moon found a dead 11 year old girl in the street turned out to be Rosie. Eventually the spiritual side of his culture reached him and helped him to ease the pain, before that he had killed dozens of people, men only and mostly lawmen. So when he said turning it into a race war was the wrong fight people were compelled to listen. When he said all cultures unite together to fight the corruption, the corruption being those in high towers and the ones who were responsible for all the loss and pain was the right fight, people were compelled to listen.

That kind of thing is exactly what judge Woodroof wanted to change. He figured that over a long enough time if the law was not honest and enough people had been cheated by it eventually, Wolf's idea would too become a reality and the hundreds of people would march the courthouse and the jail house and tear them down and in doing so tear down the law in the town. He believed that the only way the people would ever have regard for the law's integrity is if the law was willing to place the highest regard on its own integrity. Hallalujah and god bless the good honorable judge. He demonstrated his integrity for all of Purgeatory to see.

There was a case of a Latino girl a while back. She was raped and beaten and didn't want to involve the law, her brothers felt otherwise they damn near beat the man to death. The man took his assault to court and during the trial referred to the Salvatina boys as already dead. He said the girl was a Latino whore who didn't have a right to refuse him, on account of her being Latino and him being the heir to the iron mine.

Judge Woodroof warned him several times and when he offered the judge a fortune during the trial right in front of everybody to hang the Salvatina boys and the sister, he had finally heard enough. He sentenced Mr Macchrystie to one week up at the jail house for contempt of court, trying to pervert the course of justice and attempt to bribe a representative of the law. He upheld the charges against the Salvatina brothers but urged the girl to press a charge of her own against Mr Macchrystie which she did.

Within one week the judge had set up a hearing for the girl and found Mr Macchrystie guilty, he was ordered to apologize and pay the girl compensation. For an heir to a large estate and huge fortune he sure was none too smart, he then proceeded to try to bribe the judge again which finally pushed Judge Woodroof over the edge. The judge added a second attempt of bribery and perversion of justice to the already long list of offenses against Mr Macchrystie and sentenced him to hang. In the days following, the Macchrystie estate attempted to amend the findings of the court and enlisted the help of three deputies and a court usher. They then proceeded to the judge's residence where they threatened him and his family. The following morning 2 days early Mr Macchrystie was hanged in an impromptu fashion along with his older brother, three deputies and a court usher who had all been implicated in the offences. Judge Woodroof had the respect of many in the town which was imperative if he was going to convince anybody that the law still worked.

    I think he knew that in order to believe in the law, people would have to be able to first believe in the people who represented it. He was exactly what Purgeatory needed, it was starting to work too. When he handed me my sentence I was smiling, I can't describe the look he gave me when he saw me smile, he asked what I was smiling at. It was mostly because he said I would be able to go with the army in the spring. That and because I would never have argued with him, I trusted his judgement like many did and if he would have said I was gonna hang then I would have accepted that too. Without the smile though!

    I didn't mind so much, it was coming up winter and I was fed up being cold all the time. The jail was the closest thing to home I had, it was warm and there was a bed. I got coffee every morning and they even fed me, daily. I hadn't eaten daily since I was a boy before my mother died and it wasn't much but it was more than I was used to, some of the other men used to complain about it, I never did. It was kind of hot sometimes and the best part was it was free and I didn't have to catch it and kill it. The days went by pretty fast for me. I used to exercise in my cell pretty much 8 – 10 hours each day, it was cool in the day and I didn't dehydrate much. When the night fell it was cold but not anything like the cold I used to experience outside.

Wasn't long now and I would be leaving with the army, there was a book at the jail house called to live and die a soldier. Regrettably I could not read like so many others, particularly the younger people but the old man in the cell opposite loved to read and when I asked him if he would read the book about the soldier out loud, I was in all honesty quite surprised he agreed.
The book thankfully detailed a soldier's life, what a soldier would expect to experience and what would be expected from him. To be honest it didn't sound that hard, didn't sound too different to an average day, for me at least.

A soldier would have to be brave even if he knew he was gonna die. Like a young boy trying to defend his dead father's house from a posse. A soldier had to be tough, most men would have a hard time adjusting to the living conditions but they would be no worse than the ones I had gotten used to. A soldier would have to fight and even kill when he is ordered to. I had a feeling that killing a man because I had been ordered to would be harder than killing a man for some more personal reason. A soldier would have to be good at taking instructions and obeying orders, I thought I might struggle with that one. The list went on but the point was, I felt like I had a real chance of being good at soldiering. Maybe if I had lived the much easier life I had longed for I would not be so confident but the last 5 – years had been incredible, impossible even and that would prepare me well for the army.

    I wasn't in pristine condition but wasn't doing too bad, was down to 1 remaining testicle, couldn't hear much in one ear. I was missing a few teeth but I was told they would grow back on account of I was still young. The few broken bones that I had picked up along the way had healed in their own time, in their own fashion. Yeah, maybe that rib wasn't the same as before and it still hurt every time it got cold, maybe my jaw didn't sit square anymore and made it hard to chew. Maybe I dragged the left leg a little when I walked and the peripheral vision in my left eye was narrower than a wood nail. But I could still outrun any man in this town. Still hold my own in a fight, even outnumbered 4 to 1 and I had survived another year and turned 16 in my cell at some point between the winter and the spring. As I keep saying, I survived.

Well the early part of spring soon rolled around and I could hear bird song in the early hours. It would only be matter of weeks now before I left this cell, left this town and started a new chapter as they say, of my life. I was trying to prepare as much as I could before I left. I had failed pretty much all of my previous to do list about reclaiming the house, paying back Mimi and making some money. But I had been getting a lot of exercise and in conjunction with eating regularly I had put on some welcome weight. Morgan's clothes no longer did the job, Eddie Sanchez brought me some clothes one morning and said they were from Issobella.

Turned out they were her late father's, he had passed since I had been in this cell.

They were lovely clothes, unfortunately they did not fit.

Was kind of funny after that different people brought me clothes, mostly they did not fit. I was long in the leg and wide across the shoulders as well as deep in the chest. Then the most unexpected thing happened, I said before life has a way of surprising me. Mark, the deputy on duty brought me an old army uniform, blue trousers and a blue shirt, they fit beautifully and I knew right away who's they were. Sgt Cedric Green had donated his old soldier's uniform to me and I was a little overcome, I will never understand why he would do that. I probly wouldn't see him again before I left but if I ever come back here I now owed him too.

12TH. INITIATION.

I'm not at all sure what day it was, it's kind of hard to keep track of time in a cell. The army recruiters arrived and I was like the coyote who found a dead buffalo, I could hardly hide my excitement. In contrast the recruiter seemed to be wholly unmoved, he was none too happy about resorting to rounding up the prisoners. I think the army was hoping for a better standard of recruits.

He took me and the old man across from me, I liked the old man he was the closest thing to friend I had. I don't think I would have made it through the first 6 months without all the help the old man gave me. I felt that it was my duty to try to help him in any way I could so we struck a kind of deal. When it came to the physical aspects of the training everybody but me found it a struggle. In contrast the more academic parts seemed to be beyond my grasp, wasn't just me that failed to comprehend those aspects.

There were a whole lot men, young and old who never learned to read. Besides the inability to read the written word many of us failed to write and often even speak them. The army made their stance pretty clear they were not school teachers. Fortunately for me however I had a means of learning these things that had thus far escaped me, the old man seemed to be well educated and by far the most academic in the group. It seemed clear to us both that if I helped him with the physical challenge this training presented to us and he helped me with the academic parts, we both had a strong chance of progressing through the first 6 months of training simply referred to as initiation.

When the deputy unlocked my cell I felt a sense of freedom like a wild animal set free. Well I tell you it didn't last long, the army recruiter was a real son of a bitch. By the time I got to the pram I was already questioning whether things had just gotten better or worse. Lieutenant Berkeley seemed to be a tougher prospect than the town jail, there was six of us in total and 4 prams. We travelled over hard scorched ground, with narrow passes between towering mountains and every direction harsh but beautifull natural scenery. All the way to Silver City passing through Inertia and Contention on the way.

My new friend was keeping his word as was the marker of an honorable man, teaching as best he could how to read, write and pronounce. That was difficult, so much stuff that was hard for most men came easy to me but those lessons did not. By the time we reached Silver City 8 or 9 days had gone by and the recruiters had rounded up as many as a dozen prisoners and vagrants. On arrival at the army office in Silver City there was ten new recruits and two dead men.

I had decided on the way that I was gonna approach this experience in a certain way. I thought back to when I had been fighting off that group of gunmen up at the Purgeatory town limits. The kind of mental toughness and single minded focus I had, I recall how in that moment I had felt like nothing could divert me from what I was intent on doing. I had a feeling that the immediate future would require large amounts of that very thing, I was adamant that I was gonna prove to them that I already had that and would not need to be taught how to be tough.

It was unexpected like so many things in life, I didn't feel full of fear or concern instead I was prepared for the forthcoming trial by fire that this experience was sure to be.

Many of the recruits used this as a way to escape a lengthy jail sentence, some just wanted to die and thought that the army ought to do the job. Either way almost every one of us was intimidated or afraid, all except me. I knew I was gonna succeed and I knew I was be accomplished at soldiering, further more I knew I would be returning home and had big plans for the future.

The Lieutenant seemed to have no part in the training his job was enlisting the new recruits, that and obviously filling us all with enthusiasm….. The responsibility for training the enlisted rested with Sgt Paris and his 2nd man, 1st class Hounsou. From day one it seemed to be tough for everybody but me, and I had mixed feelings about that. Of course I was thrilled that I was so capable but on the other hand even I had noticed that I was starting to stand out.

Even at my young years I knew very well what standing out meant, all those many years ago when I used to labor for my father he was keen for me to learn woodwork. I have a clear memory of measuring cutting and nailing wooden boards for the bull shed and fence, I remember him telling me each board needed 3 nails at each end. He would start off all 3 first so he could make sure they were where he wanted them, then go back hammer them all the way in one at a time. I used to watch the way he did it so that I knew what to do when it was my turn.

After he hit the first 2 nails, the third stood out all by its self, it looked so vulnerable like it had no way of hiding. It's just something I remember. I was like that third nail had been all my life, standing out or on my own or no way of hiding what I was. I thought that maybe this experience would be a good time for me to learn how to blend in a bit more or at least stand out a bit less.

The 1st class had punishments for recruits who he felt were not trying hard enough or had a poor attitude toward the training. The Sgt had punishments for the recruit's full stop. Not long after we first arrived at the army training camp we were all lined up in a row, the Lt, was asking us why we joined and what we could offer the army. The first guy was only at the front because he was in so much of a hurry to get inside to see whether they had water, he was going on about it all the way there. It was that really which had led to his unfortunate hanging upside down, when the Lt asked him why he had joined the army, he told the truth. He wanted to escape 8 more years in that cell. That went over like horse shit for a wedding gift. When the Lt was done screaming at him he was passed over to the Sgt. I could tell right then by the look the Sgt gave him his life was gonna be hell for the next 6 months. The rest of us had learnt from his debasing that this was one of those times that you ought not to tell the truth.

We were about a week in, not sure really. Bait as he was now known, that was the waterman. Had been singled out from the start and was not having a good time. The Sgt did that every group that came through here. Gave us all unimaginative and derogatory names, mine was {half-breed}, among the others were Toothless, Flatnose, Pig and Whitehair the reasons for these nicknames were rather obvious. I got the sense that the Sgt had been after Bait since day one and was waiting for an opportunity, he seemed over excited when his opportunity came.

Bait had not improved since he got here, it was our responsibility to improve during the first week and then each week thereafter. He was unable to complete even the most basic physical drills whilst he was not alone in that, he was alone in that he had shown no progress at all in the first week. Since day one I was first to complete every physical task not surprising, I was the youngest. Some of the men who couldn't complete the physical tasks at the beginning had improved enough to do so by now. The Sgt had said that Mathew was only ever gonna be good for one thing, Bait. When he failed to complete the drill at the end of the first week and had not even shown any improvement, the Sgt ordered to the rest of us that we build a wooden cross. To a few of us it was clear what was gonna happen, I was put up for the project due to having experience with wood working. Three of us constructed a cross made out of wooden boards and nailed it to a strong square base so that it would stand. When the Sgt came to inspect the project he seemed pleased and was uncharacteristically complimentary. He ordered only one change that the cross was to be placed upside down.

During the night the Sgt, the 1st class and one other man came out of nowhere and ambushed the whole group, they took Bait and left. As they were leaving they commanded that we did not follow them, so we stayed put. The following morning we walked from where we had been sleeping to the exercise yard just like every other morning except this time there was only nine of us and when we reached the exercise yard we found the 10th man. He was stripped naked and tied upside down to the cross that I and two other recruits had made, he had clearly been there all night. I wasn't at all affected by this but the other two men seemed perturbed, it was clear in my head that he was not hanging there because I had made the cross. He was there because he was a good for nothing, lazy, bone idle son of a bitch.

When I was building the cross the other two men kept speculating and questioning I wasn't interested in that I just kept thinking about the damn nails, I used the same technique as my father taught me when I was a boy. I hit the first nail all the way in then as my attention turned to the second nail I thought that Bait was obviously the third nail at the moment. The one that stands out but if he died then there would have to be someone else who would take over from him someone else who would then stand out. That person who ever it was would be like the second nail, safe as long as the third nail stood out. I didn't want to become the next nail to stand out and I knew that I didn't have to be the best in the group, I just had to be better than the next worse so I started looking around at the rest of the group.

I figured Pig was pretty poor and kept failing physical. I knew the Sgt was already looking at him and possibly even one other. I had gotten pretty good at reading people's facial expressions since I started years ago when I first went to town. The old man understandably lacked in the physical department and I had been trying to help by working beside him and slowing down so that he could try to work to my pace and then spurring him on. Whilst Bait and Pig were around he would be safe but I reckoned he would be next in line after that.

Bait had passed out at first I thought he was dead. The 1st class was quick to point out that blood has been flowing to his head on account of him hanging upside down, it had been the excess blood in his head that had made him pass out. Didn't know it at the time but that would be one of many things I learnt in the army that I would employ later in life.

13TH. PASSED THE TEST.

The business with Bait went on for a while until one day in training he pulled Hounsou's pistol from his belt assumedly with the intention to use it, my money was on either the Sgt or the 1st class himself. Didn't come to that not too much of a stretch of the imagination to conceive that the 1st class might be quicker and stronger than Bait was, anyway before Bait could get the thing sat right in his hand Hounsou took it off him and then broke his neck.

We were down to nine, I guessed that Pig would now be the main subject of scrutiny, a couple of the recruits were disturbed by witnessing Hounsou kill Bait; I was not. I think I understood that he died because he wasn't trying. He was just using the army as a way to escape the prison term he had been handed, rightly so on account of the crime he confessed. Didn't know what that crime was but I got the sense that it was something disgusting due to the remarks the Sgt used to make. Bait committed a horrible offence then tried to escape his sentence. He insulted the army and everything it stood for by coming here like it was a holiday camp and whilst some were working as hard as they could he was taking it easy. Not wanting to commit not wanting to even try. But as if that wasn't bad enough he reached for Housou's side arm. I cannot think of any way he could be defended in this. No way to mitigate the circumstances that led to his execution, which is what it was.

The Sgt is not a stupid man nor the 1st class for that matter, it was not happenstance that led Bait to reach for the gun. I watched the whole thing unwrap in front of me. They could see Bait was wearing thin like he might be on the verge or like a breaking point that would not be acceptable for the unit. When I think about it, how could it? He would have constantly jeopardized the whole unit and worse, threatened the integrity of the Sgt, the unit and the army.

No, I did not have any sympathy for him to my mind Bait got Bait killed and deserved everything he got.

It was no mystery to me that if a man does well, he will be well rewarded but if he does poorly then poor is what he will be. I like to think that I have learnt something from every experience I have had, I certainly learned from this one. How far will the Sgt go to filter out any one who is a threat to the unit, a threat to the army or even just its reputation? As far as he needs to. Seemed to me that for any man who was onboard with the agenda and willing to commit to it, work for it. There would be no need to find himself in disfavor with the Sgt.

It rained hard all night, I didn't get any sleep and I assume that was true for the rest of the group. I was soaked through all night, cold and shivering. We all were and the mood in the camp continued to deteriorate. I like to think that I had learned enough by now to be able to make a pretty accurate assessment of each situation I would find myself in out here. That said I was not expecting any leniency or sympathy in the morning, well I was right about that much at least. By the time the sun came up in the morning I was frozen through just like the old days, except this time it seemed to bother me more than I remember it use to. I thought about how long I had been in a warm, dry cell. I knew instantly that being inside for so long had spoilt me, made me soft. Now I was defiant and if memory serves me correct, that is when I was most focused, most determined.

It was a fortunate coincidence that I was going to be determined and defiant that day, once again I was ahead of the curve. I knew there would be physical at some point and hoped that it would be sooner rather than later. I couldn't get out of these wet clothes and into a nice warm dry uniform but that didn't mean I had to be shivering and cold all day long. If I just started exercising I would start to get warm. I lined up just like always but decided that instead of waiting to be instructed I was gonna get moving, been doing this long enough now I knew the routine. I noticed I was getting some attention from the other recruits, wondered if any of them would catch on. The private 1st class, Housou walked over to me and truthfully I was expecting the heel of his boot, instead he just stood there watching and didn't say anything.

The Sgt arrived and no doubt noticed the other men standing there cold and shaking. I continued my workout when the 1st class was standing there but only until the Sgt arrived; when he got there I stood to attention.

On the plus side I was no longer cold or shivering, he looked at me and asked me why I stopped. Well I said "I didn't know what to do so I did what we do every morning, figuring that to be right." He asked me if I recall anybody asking me to stop so what else could I do! I started up with the routine again. The Sgt seemed somewhat more relaxed than usual for the remainder of that day. I'm not at all sure whether he was pleased that I started by myself or not but he asked the rest of the group if they were waiting for something in particular, they got started soon after. I was getting the sense that this initiation thing was not as difficult as we had all thought it was. I mean I could have been hung upside down for all I knew but instead they seemed to welcome it and just kind of followed my lead.

In the coming weeks the mood seemed to ease up a little. I didn't do the whole starting in my own time thing again, wasn't sure whether I should be doing it or not but felt that I would be pushing my luck. Sometime in the early part of the summer they finally filtered out Pig, to be honest I was surprised it took so long. I thought that he would have been gone a long time ago, he really dug in after Bait was killed. That's what I been trying to say, I know what happened was a bit extreme but it did have the right affect on the group. I learnt that lesson well, if it saved the lives of another nine soldiers then the sacrifice of one man's life would be quite acceptable. It was simple here, much simpler than Purgeatory anyway. Learn from your experiences, commit to the agenda and work hard that was all you had to do. The army didn't want to carry passengers. It had no interest in people who would always need to be told what to do

next and was not going to help the unfortunate with a personal development program.
Wasn't really that difficult and was not at all complicated, well not any more at least. After Pig died we were down to eight men and my concern was that the old man was the next weakest.

It wasn't long before it came around. The old man was always committed and I think it was pretty obvious that he was doing the best he could, now the problem became something else. We had been over how the army didn't want people who were not committed or were not trying and that remains true. It is also true that even a man who has the right attitude and may well be respected for that, is still a liability if he is not physically good enough. I put myself on the cross just one time in his place, I figured I owed him that much.

I could see he was struggling and Hounsou was already shouting at him, we had been here twice before by now so I knew what was coming. I pretended to be unable to finish and predictably he soon turned his attention to me. Yeah they put me up on the cross. It wasn't so bad really, I had a terrible headache but really other than that the experience was not as bad as I thought. I got the sense that Hounsou knew why I did what I did, it remained to be seen whether he would respect me for it or chastise me for it. Had a feeling that the way things were around here it wouldn't be long before I found out. Sun came up that morning and I was awake to see it. I think I did pass out late in the night but had come to again at some point. I thought I had an answer to my question about whether I would be chastised for my actions yesterday, seeing as they didn't put me up here naked and they let me keep my underwear. After they pulled me down it went pretty much back to normal, was just like any other day. We didn't really speak about it but I felt that it was understood by all.

    We were all men, black, white, native or Latino it didn't matter here. We seemed to instinctively understand each other. I had taken a bullet for a fellow soldier, given him another chance. My record had been unmarked until that point so I could afford one misdemeanor whereas the old man had been warned more than once. I could give him one but I could not do it again.

The next time it came around I was concerned for the old man as I knew I could not help this time. I have said many times that life has a way of surprising me and that the unexpected often turns out to be the best outcome. Luke Warren a tall skinny black man was another who had been pretty safe until now. Did the strangest thing, he failed to come up from the ground during exercise. I knew what he was doing because that is exactly what I had done, he spent the night on the cross. We were about 5 months in I guess, hard to say for sure. I was thinking that we had a chance to get all eight of us through initiation and if we did we would form a unit.

By now we had been noticing a kind of unity in the group, it didn't feel like a bunch of individual people anymore. It had started to feel like a unit, the next time the 1st class set out for the old man he stopped short and looked down the line. He looked square at every one of us. I guess he knew what was coming, he was waiting to see if anybody else would step forward for the old man.

Hulio Garcia stepped forward and dropped to the floor, he complained that he would not be able to complete basic today and was tired. So he spent the night on the cross. He was welcomed back to the group the following morning just like Warren had been. I don't know about anybody else but I personally was overwhelmed with a sudden emotion. Warren and Garcia felt like heroes and I was expecting a fallout from our actions as a group, I think I missed an intricate point. We were supposed to be developing a sense of responsibility, becoming leaders and we were. Although we had gone against the Sgt we had gone along with the agenda. Taking responsibility for each other and ourselves and demonstrating a willingness to go out of our way for our fellow soldiers. I guess we didn't realize it at the time but we were doing exactly what they wanted us to do, we were growing as soldiers and as men.

Quite unexpectedly we turned out to be one of the better groups in recent years. In doing so we were granted the honor of forming our own unit. We were to become the Contention City Guard, 2nd unit in the coming weeks. By the final week of initiation we were no longer undesirables, no longer a bunch of criminals and vagrants. We had become something more, we had become soldiers proud and selfless. The physical stopped by the last week of training as a group we had made it that far. Four of us had bought the old man's way to the final week in return for all he had done for us. He was the only one of us able to read and the army were clear they had no time to teach us. He did have time and did all he could to teach us as much as he could in the short time available. He also pointed out potential traps before we stepped into them. In truth he had done as much to keep us alive as we had done for him. I think we were pretty unanimous in hoping he would be the unit's leader. I personally was relieved when he was announced, I recall he had the keenest smile on his face. Hounsou shook his hand

and told him he had a great unit and that we now had to earn our place, had to give back to the army and America.

The thought of me fighting for something other than just to survive thrilled me, I was used to fighting for my life but it never really made sense to me why I did it or what I was fighting for. I had longed for some transparent, justifiable cause to fight for. I had no problem with dying but I wanted to know what I was dying for, desperately wanted a reason to keep fighting. I hadn't presumed to be gifted with that in the army. I had come here to improve myself and maybe if it's not asking too much even prove myself but never thought I would get all that and the thing I wished for the most, some good reason for all the suffering and to keep fighting.

Well we had completed initiation and formed a unit. We had a company and a responsibility, next we were assigned an office in Contention and each of us issued with a side arm. There was no going back now whatever the future it would never be like it was before. I was a soldier and intended to be the best soldier I could be. I will also take with me something private 1st class said to us before we left, "out there you might be white or black, Latino or native and maybe you think the world see's you differently. To the army you are all the same, the army doesn't care what color you are or who your god is. You all bleed the same to the army, you all die the same to the army. Die for the army and you will be decorated, you will be honored and remembered as a man." That sounded fine by me and I was preparing to leave here and journey to the future as a man, as a soldier.

14ᵀᴴ. INTO THE FUTURE.

The days went by on our way to Contention we stopped on a night just outside the town of Red Sands. We were hungry and tired, two of us were sent out to find some food, two others set up a fire around which we would camp. The old man put a detail of the three remaining men on guarding the perimeter, in truth they were guarding something so much more important than that. There was only one deed for all of our business in Contention. It was the deed to the city office and also it detailed our jurisdiction, our responsibilities and arguably most important of all our pay, besides other things. The old man had it and he was trying to guard it as well as he could but I personally felt like he had taken some unnecessary risks with the document. Sending two men into town left only six. Two men making a fire are not armed and prepared to fight that leaves four. We had been lucky so far to have come all the way to Red Sands with the deed, horses, guns and our lives intact. The trouble with luck as Ed Henry always says is luck runs out. This inescapable fact was wearing weary on my mind, I was tired and my patience was wearing thin.

When I was dispatched with Warren into Red Sands, I strongly protested and had to speak my mind. Either Warren or myself would be capable of hunting on our own. I pointed out that losing two men now would leave the unit vulnerable. The old man was a class act it was obvious he didn't agree with my point of view but the group felt it was in the best interest so he agreed. I was sent alone into town and was not enthusiastic about my responsibility.
I would have to try to find supplies, alcohol and medicines stuff like that. Without having any money to pay with and just convince the store keeper that we had a city office in Contention and when we took office we would settle up our affairs. The second part of my job was to hunt for food on the way back. I was less apprehensive

about that although having said that, I have not seen a deer or a fox or even a rabbit for days now.

When I arrived in Red Sands, the first thing I noticed was that there seemed not to be a sheriff or city marshal in town. There was a jail house but it was empty. There was a trail of blood outside the saloon that lead all the way to the stables. I knew then why the town was called Red Sands. I tried the stores but it was no good. I wasn't getting anywhere and it wasn't just because I failed to be convincing but mostly because the store keepers I encountered seemed too afraid to even talk to me. I would be lying if I said I didn't know how this was gonna play out. Something had gotten the whole town rattled, I was betting I would find it at the saloon.

I got to the saloon just in time to see for myself. A native man stood in the middle of the room. There were three men surrounding him, I had seen this game before I was not amused then I would not be amused now. The idea of the game was each of the four men would get 1 bullet, then each man would spin the chamber before firing. I ordered a beer sat at the bar it was obvious that those three men were part of whatever posse had a grip of the town. The first man span his barrel then fired. I was watching the old native man, I was no expert but I think that scarf was Navaho. He shut his eyes tight and kind of cringed every time the men took a shot at him. Then when they had all fired and it was his turn he tentatively spun the barrel then fired aimlessly demonstrating no real intent.

    I looked around the room for a while and slowly drank my beer. The people were gathered around a few old, worn, circular wooden tables and some were sat facing sideways so they could look away more easily. There were men and women sat at some tables in two's and three's. There was one table with four dusty men, intensely watching the cruel game. There were all kinds of faces in the bar. Some sad and afraid. Some eager for the Navaho man to get shot and some looked angry and vengeful, those are the ones I was interested in. Those are the men who want to do something about it but are too afraid. The point there being that if somebody else acted and they became less afraid they might just take a stand.

I had an idea how I might be able to get those supplies. I'd say it was a bad idea but didn't seem much point. It was my idea, all of my ideas were bad ideas. I felt for the Navaho, I know how proud their kind are and I guess those men did too and that is why they were doing it. An attempt to strip him of his pride before they kill him. I tried to read the room but I wasn't sure which way it would go. If I did something would it set the whole bar off like igniting dynamite or would it inspire the angry people to act. I couldn't make it too obvious as I was unsure. The old Navaho made it to round 5 then one of the outlaws shot him dead. They were standing around laughing about it and taunting the young Navaho woman who I assumed was with him.

They grabbed her and started tearing at her clothes. I finished my beer turned toward them and stood up. All that tearing at her clothes exposed her chest I took one last look around the room to see if anybody else had balls. Well I guess not, she was stood there bare chested and tearful. I couldn't help notice how good she looked both brave and vulnerable. Tearful yet still proud. Her hair unorganized and her dress torn, she would never look this perfect again.

I almost forgot I had to do something, I picked up the gun from the dead Navaho and checked it just to make sure it was loaded. I put the barrel back and took position in the center of the bar just like the dead man. I called out, "you fellers wanna play again?" They turned to look at me and whilst they had turned attention from the girl I looked at her. She looked right into my eyes and I tried to subtly gesture toward her to exit undetected.

The fools gathered around me. I could tell the type, poor personal hygiene, dirty clothes and unchecked facial hair. It took three of them just to kill a poor old man and their treatment of the girl was confirmation. It was all the usual bullshit empty threats and childish insults. I had a mind to just shoot 'em and get on with my business but I didn't wanna cheat. I knew I was gonna need the town for those supplies. The one who killed the old native man was either too drunk or too stupid to even realize he hadn't reloaded his gun, I have had worse odds.

The first one spun his barrel and fired. I had decided I wasn't gonna flinch, I didn't. I looked the son bitch right in the eye. Then the next man, again I didn't flinch. Then my turn, I made a point of aiming it right at his head. I looked him square in the eye. The next round came and went without incident but the third round was unlucky for me and them. The first shot I knew wasn't gonna come to anything, he was the man firing an empty pistol. The second shot hit me right in the shoulder, not the first time I been shot, won't be the last. They began to celebrate a little too soon my turn came round. I am very happy to say I shot one of the men in the head.

I'm not gonna lie about the pain I felt from my shoulder but I had that single mindedness again. I could pretty much switch it on and off by now, I had another quick look around the room. Some of the men had their hands down under the table and I wondered if they were loading a gun. Then I wondered if they were part of the gang or not. Still, it looked a lot more like some of the other men might be prepared to act. I knew the rules and I was supposed to get another bullet. I knew they would not play fair but it didn't matter I had my side arm tucked discreetly into my jeans.

    I took my side arm and as I started taking out bullets and putting them in my pocket some of the men in the bar noticed it was army issue. By now I was sure I had won over the room. Was starting to get a little light headed now, round 4 and came and went. Then it was my turn and the other two men didn't want to play anymore. I knew they were not alone and had been looking round the room for the rest of their posse but I still couldn't clearly make them out.

When the remaining two men tried to quit the game, I was forced to end the charade and in doing so exposed the rest of the gang.

I had to improvise on account of I only had 1 bullet.

I grabbed the skinny one, he was the closer of the two and dragged him in front of me. I grabbed his hand and pointed his pistol at the other man. I fired off 2 shots before I hit him.
The one of the tables that had the four men sitting at it. When they stood up I knew they were the ones and the leader would be one of them. I dropped his pistol and grabbed mine the man I was using as a shield took a lot of bullets. I aimed at one of them and pulled on the trigger eventually I hit him, back to three on one. My side arm was in my right hand and the bullets in my left pocket I wasn't gonna get anywhere like that. I needed a chance to load my pistol.

I was pretty much holding the dead body that gave me an idea, I walked the body toward them and when I got closer I pushed it into the table and fled quickly behind the nearest wall.
I didn't have long before they started shooting at me. One of the bullets hit me, hurt like hell but I didn't need long to load a

standard issue 212, had done it hundreds of times in training.
I planned to dive out from behind the wall, land on the floor facing them and open up on them one at a time. In truth I fell out from behind the wall landing on the floor facing somewhere near the table and fired lower than I planned under the table. It worked out somehow, I put one in the wall behind them. One in the table leg then as the table collapsed, I finally started hitting my targets. While I was behind the wall they had separated, two remained at the table and one ran toward the side exit. I hit the two at the table then tried to find the last man. He didn't even fire on me just ran out the door. I was relieved and grateful for the end of the fire fight.

    I stood up and had planned to walk to the bar, order another beer and sit down at the bar on one of those stools, keeping my composure and maintaining my pride and dignity the whole time. If only things turned out the way I plan them. I just noticed the girl come back in through the front door with another native man. I put my chin up and my shoulders back, took one step and crashed through a table in clear sight of everyone, bounced my head off the floor and passed out. Not the dignified ending I was hoping for, what happened to me after that I don't know.

I woke up in agony the following morning in a strange bed, in a strange room where the bright sunlight came through the window and illuminated the flawless figure in the door way.
The smell of incense and the smoke in the room made me think of my mother but only for a moment until my attention was focused on the figure in the door way. She never did tell me her name but whoever she was I will remember her face, her hair, her voice, her body and her smell as well as the 2 days spent in her care with my last breath. In my final moment I will think only of her.

I was lying naked in assumedly her bed, though I tried not to I couldn't help rise.
She stepped forward out of the light and I could clearly see her face, she wore a smile.

There was a brightness in her eyes and her hair half covered her bare chest, only one breast was visible but I could cleary see how pretty she was. It didn't hang like a teardrop, just sat upon her chest like a cherry upon a cake. I cast my gaze down from her face to her chest and then lower again from her chest to the rest of her body. At her ribcage she was thin but still a healthy woman, her waist more slender and then at her hips back out again before tapering inwards for the final time for her long slender legs.

Time's like that I wish I could paint, I would have painted my fondest memories. Of which this was right at the top, I could try to descrie her silhouette in the backlight illumination but it would nor suffice. I was trying to take it all in and in no hurry to reach her feet. I was entirely overwhelmed. That was the first time I had seen a woman bare all and was completely unprepared. She was perfect everywhere and made me feel at least a dozen feelings all at once. My heart was beating so hard I thought it might leave my chest, it could cope with poison, venom and being shot but this!

She didn't speak a word. She stepped forward and pulled the blanket off me leaving me exposed, knelt on the bed looking right into my eyes and smiling at me the whole time. As she leant forward and kissed me, she threw one leg over me and sat down. If I died in that moment so be it I would have died happy. I had no idea what it would feel like or the other sensations I would experience, not just physical but emotional and sensory also. If I tried a thousand times, I would remain hopelessly unable to describe what it was like.

There was a resistance at first and I was concerned, I didn't know anything about sex.
Maybe it meant that we couldn't go any further. She put 2 of her fingers into her mouth just past her beautifull lips and place them upon her tongue. Looking right at me the whole time, teasingly sucked her fingers then moved her hand down leaning slightly forward. I flinched when I felt her fingers touch me, was only brief but it was

extremely sensitive. I could feel she put her wet fingers either side of me and touched herself. After that placed both her hands flat on my chest and sat back. As she lowered down on to me I felt the resistence give way and I began to enter her slowly, she eventually came to rest sitting on my pelvis. I was all the way in, I placed my hands on her waist just above her hips. My body ached with sensations of pleasure and my heart ached with passion and lust.

    I had no defense against powers such as these. As I lay there helpless I knew, all my life however long that may be, this would be my weakness. I laid there under her then she sat up and began to do her thing, all I could do was kiss her and grab at her. I would catch a glimpse of her eyes, then her hair would tease the concealing of them. She would just roll her eyes upward and bite her bottom lip then lean forward and kiss me. I had no idea a person could feel so many intense feelings, never mind all at the same time. My body was pulsing with an electric sensation that came to rest just below my stomach. I could not take my hands off her, could not take my eyes of her. Still can't to this day get my mind off her, her skin began to glisten as she lightly perspired, my hands finally came to rest upon her hips.

Though she didn't speak, I heard her voice as she began to moan softly which was another new experience for me and another one that completely overwhelmed. How soft her voice was as she expressed pleasure meant so much to me. She got faster gradually until the end at which point she slowed down and stopped. Given that I was already entirely overwhelmed before that it had come to a point where I could no longer cope. I held her hot shimmering body with my hands as she slowly moved forward and back, softly moaning and holding her hair out of the way of her face with one hand. The other clutching at one of her breast, I experienced the most powerful, most incredible sensation available to a man.

My whole body tense up real hard starting at my core, then a sensation ran through my body into my groin. We gazed into each other's eyes and I just could not hold on 1 second longer. We did not break eye contact, she smiled at me and placed her hands on my chest, she leant slightly forward and I pushed with my hands around her hips, her body toward mine and at the same time thrust my body upward toward her. She gasped a little, then rolled her eyes, in that moment I prayed it would never end.

I spent that and one more day there with her before I left Red Sands with the provisions I required and went in search of the unit. Those 2 days were the outstanding moments of my life and if there is a heaven for me after my death then it can only be in that room with her. I left the town of Red Sands with the medicines, alcohol and other provisions I had been tasked with getting. I didn't know if the unit would still be there or even if they were still alive, if I'm honest I did not have any feeling about it either way. I could think of nothing else other than her and could feel nothing else other than I wanted more than anything to go back to that town, to that room, to her.

I rendezvoused with the rest of the unit and attention quickly turned to the supplies.
Truthfully I think they were supprised to see me that I chose to take as a sign that they had assumed I was dead. I explained how I came about them, the supplies I mean. Everything up to the girl that was not for sharing. They said that a man came riding past a few nights ago in a hurry as if he was running from something. After we agreed that he was the man who fled the saloon, we determined that he would most likely have been on his way to rally the rest of his posse which I stated would mean retaliation for the town. Then I announced that we had a duty to stop them before they could get to the town and cause any more trouble. What I really meant was before they could get anywhere near the girl. We set out the following morning in the direction they said he had ran. I did not sleep that night at all and just kept staring at the town thinking of her, wondering what she was doing and who she was doing it with. I just wanted to go

back and nearly did twice in the night but I knew I could not.

The following morning when we set out we didn't have to wait very long before we came across the posse heading for town. My hands were shaking, adrenaline coursing through my body. Those silly bastard's, what were they thinking. If they thought they could just go back there and do what they wanted, then they had a tough lesson to learn and I was gonna make sure they learned it, hard! I recognized the man from the bar that was all I needed. I wasn't prepared to take any risks and there would be no games this time. You know, it's a strange sensation and I have come across nothing else like it. The sensation of talking to a man you know will be dead when the conversation ends, dead by your own hand.

I fired first, I got three of them myself. I broke away from the rest of the unit and took the fight toward the posse. I knew that this fight was more personal than duty so I didn't want anybody else to get shot or god forbid even killed. We got them all this time nobody got away to rally more men, fortunately my plan to break away from the unit worked and nobody got injured. I had to answer a lot of questions afterwards and found answering them difficult, despite that my fellow soldiers seemed to be wholly in support which meant a lot to me. Just a few more days until we hit Contention who knows what the next few days has planned for us.

15TH. A SPIRITUAL JOURNEY.

We got to a hill that looked down on Contention City. I didn't want to mention it but the past few days the pain I had been in had gotten worse. The old man decided it was too late in the day to find our office and get settled in as it would be dark soon. When he said we should rest for the night then go get started tomorrow morning, I had to take the opportunity to do something about the pain I was in. I went to speak to him to tell him that I was gonna go ahead and do some reconnaissance for tomorrow. He didn't like me keep heading off on my own and not doing what he said and I had to be honest I knew it was bad because the others noticed. It was constantly undermining him, countermanding his orders and I was sorry for that. I had come to terms with it and decided that as soon as I got some help with this pain I was in, I would turn to following instructions like everybody else. At the time

I was clearly in a lot of pain although I tried to hide it. He looked at me funny and though he agreed, I got the sense that he knew it was not about reconnaissance.

    I wandered off in the direction of another new town, another unknown. The trouble with the unknown is that the immediate future is somewhat pre-determined. I'm sure that our actions change things, even if not as much as we like to think but whatever is supposed to happen is gonna happen one way or another even if not exactly how it was determined to. I didn't feel at all strong but I still had to accept that there was a plan for my arriving in Contention that night ahead of the rest of my unit. Impossible to say whether it would be getting shot, maybe even killed or having another glorious experience like the one I had just a few night past, maybe it was both. Wasn't really up to it either way but that didn't change anything. I was learning that life wasn't a game of choices, more like a series of tests.

Didn't really seem to matter if we are prepared or not it's gonna happen anyway.

Thinking of life and all of its events in this way seemed to work for me. Used to try to just take one test at a time with the plan being not to fail. Whether I failed or not didn't bother me anymore, all that mattered now was facing each test head on, prepared or not.

    I got into town and tied up my horse outside the drug store. As I was entering the store an old native man who was leaving at the time looked right at me, his eyes locked on me as we walked past each other. Again I am not an expert on such matters however, it seemed to me that he was Apache and reminded me in some way of my mother. I asked the counter clerk for painkillers, the strongest he had. He put something or other down on the counter and then wanted to charge me. I supposed that the whole I'm with the army and we have an office right across the street, I have my name on a deed that says the city will pay me wages each week by the end of the week I will come back and pay for the painkillers speech would turn out to be little more than a waste of time. I just took them, gave him a cold stare and put the noisy end of my side arm in his face. Not the way I like to do things but I was in a lot of pain and in no mood to fuck around.

I left the store and when I got outside the Apache man was talking to my horse. I didn't pull my gun on him, I knew better than that. I have known all my life that you can't pull a gun on he's people and can't force their participation with fear, you get a lot more from them if you respect them and their ways. I asked him what he wanted, he never did answer that question. I felt like I was dying, not for the first time. He gave me a short speech about he could see that my spirit was native, very old native. I still wasn't in the mood for fucking about and fully intended to ridicule him, I asked him how he knew that? He said he could see it clear as he could see me which was unusual, said he'd never seen a spirit so clearly before.

"You can see my spirit?" I mocked him rudely, I should not have done. "I can see it so clearly because it's about to leave your body", when he said that I felt a chill deep inside my body. I was cold and weak and could feel that I was getting weaker, I was done mocking him.

"You saying I'm dying?" "You ask questions when you already know the answers." I knew it was true, I had done for a while. "I look at you I see 2 things. One is a dead man and the other is a glowing golden spirit as strong as the bull and as wise as the wolf. Old like these lands are, if only your body could know what your spirit knows or have the strength it does." I didn't know what to say, "Well I guess that glowing spirit will be free soon, free of this dying body." "No you must not! This is not when your body is supposed to die." "If what you say is true, I don't have a choice and there is nothing I can do about it." "There is something that can be done but you must come with me and you must release control of yourself completely and give yourself wholly." I agreed, didn't seem like I had much choice.

    He led me away into the mountains but in truth by the time I got there I was pretty much incapable of remembering the journey or riding the horse or even speaking. His horse was leading mine. All of my effort went into just keeping my body upright on the back of that horse. In town I had no idea just how close I was to dying or how quickly I would get there.

I was in and out of consciousness when we got to wherever it was we were going. I could feel that somebody pulled me off my horse and laid me down on the ground and I could hear talking but could not understand it or even focus on the voices. I could see nothing at all and could not open my eyes. I made out the smell of incense burning and that was the last of my senses.

As far as I know I passed out at that moment but what happened after is unexplainable and so far removed from the ordinary, so fantastic that I doubt it was real. I would say that I dreamed it whilst I slept after passing out. If not for the man who brought me here and a few others describing in detail exactly what I had experienced in my dream. Perhaps there is a simple explanation which I have yet to determine or perhaps it all happened and they who were in the room witnessed it first hand, either way I was not keen to draw conclusions. One conclusion I can come to however, it appears at some point during the night my heart stopped.

My mind wandered off outside the confines of my consciousness where I saw a vision. Some of the details of which are hazy, others are so clear I could swear that they were real and I was really there.

It's all a little incredible and I won't protest if you dismiss it all as fantastic, I'm gonna have to ask you to bear with me. I woke completely free from pain and seemed to have forgotten whatever it was that had been bothering me. I felt different, not sure how so but I could see and hear just fine, excellent actually! Better than I had done in years. Everything seemed so clear, I wasn't juggling concerns and problems like I can remember doing. Even though I could not recall what any of those concerns were. Movement seemed odd wasn't like walking, was more like I looked at a specific place and thought of myself as being there and then I was there and could look back at where I had just been. It seemed to be a forest which for a boy from the hard, dry desert was kind of hard to accept. I knew what a forest was and knew there were places on the great earth where they existed but had reason to believe that I was standing in one.

I made my way through the supposed forest for a short while until I came to the top of a hill or maybe it wasn't a hill, I'm not sure. It was like an enormous hill but with steps and it was made of stone. At the top I stood over a fire and looked down on the flat land surrounding the stone hill. As far I could see in all directions there was nothing but dense forest, streams and waterfalls. But a large area around the stone hill was flat sand just like home. It was covered with lots more, much smaller hills made from stone and the whole area was populated with people.

They were most odd looking, some were wearing what looked like skirts while others wore what I can only describe as underwear. They were all topless men and women alike.

They wore more on top of their head than on their body. Large head dresses made of green and gold feathers and leaves more than a foot tall. Their faces and torso's were painted. I can remember it clearly, it looked like they were all dancing and making a lot of noise; not sure maybe singing or some kind of chanting. Up on the hill there were others around me right and left, they were not singing and their head dresses seemed somehow more elaborate and taller.

    My body was tall and skinny. I remember clearly that it bore many scars and was partially painted with gold, I had a knife in one hand. The knife seemed unproportionately large. It was long but not wide and I don't know whether it was my mental state at the time or the knife but I recall the blade not being straight more like waves. I cut my other hand with the knife and then purposefully bled into the fire, the flames rose up and engulfed my hand yet I did not remove it from the fire. I looked at my hand it was not burnt, it looked like the cut had been cauterized but somehow without burning the hand. I confess to knowing nothing about it or the culture or their language yet it seemed to be ceremonious.

I can remember what the weather was like, still, dry and hot with bright sunshine a lovely day. In my vision I put my hands up toward the sky in an open arm and open hand gesture, I could see that many others did also. Just then a single flash of lightning shot across the sky, it began to thunder then the sky darkened and finally it began raining heavily. The people on the ground continued to dance. I sat in a large chair made of dark wood and detailed with gold. I seem to recall a feeling it's hard to describe it exactly but it was as if I was invincible. I felt so strong and confident like I was prepared for anything, like nothing scared or intimidated me and like what ever there was to threaten or challenge me in that world or any other I believed in my ability to defeat it. The last thing I remember is thinking it was a ceremony for the gods but if a man could have that much strength who needed the gods?

I woke for real after that and found that I was laying on a rug in a tent surrounded by what I thought was Apache men and women. They were not Apache, in fact they were called Anasazi. I had only ever heard that name once. My mother spoke of them to my father long time ago. She said that when she was just a girl and her father was sick he got help from an ancient tribe called the Anasazi. The legend stated that they were men and women but they were different to regular people and they didn't age like everyone else did. An Anasazi man or woman could live a hundred years without ageing a day. Also that their lives existed in all of the past, present and future in the way that our lives did in our own present.

The old Anasazi man who brought me here spoke of my dream in detail like it was his own. He, as well as some of the others in the room were adamant that is was not a dream.
That I had passed from the realm of the living as my body had expired and wandered into the realm of something else which

exists somewhere else and there I had seen a vision of my previous life and seeing how strong I had been managed to find my way back to this life, to my body. Well I don't know about that, it would make a great story to tell my boy if ever I had one but other than that I found it hard to accept. I was sure that they had given me medicine or some other form of treatment but they insisted they had not that all they had done was opened a doorway for me and then accompanied me on the journey so that they could guide me. They swore they had seen everything I saw as I saw it. Well whatever they did I am eternally grateful to them.

    The old Anasazi man who called himself Sagamaw showed me the path back to the town. Before I rode away he asked me why I had come here. I said I was with the army and we had an office in the city, he knew that but asked me again why had I come here? I didn't know, not really. I guessed at a couple reasons like wanted to grow strong or wanted to prove myself. There was of course the obvious reason, money. He said they were not the reason I was there but didn't tell me what the reason was. I assume he knew the reason although I don't feel entirely comfortable with somebody knowing and I do not.

In the meantime the rest of the unit had checked in to the office and pretty much completed the business of registering our credentials with the city mayor. We were all due a pay check at the end of the week and on that subject I'm glad the old man was in charge what with him being the only one who could read and write and all. Cause he said he noticed an error on the ledger in the mayor's office. Error of course just being another way of saying they were trying to cheat us out of pay, no surprises so far. Funny how things work out. If we had come all the way here without the old man we would never had noticed that error or the several others he discovered in the coming weeks. Of course when we tried to help him back in initiation, it was not motivated by what he might be able to do for us in the future but rather because we liked him and he had helped us.

When I got back to town I noticed Warren moving things into the office. I was pleased that they had completed the business of moving in without too much trouble. I walked into the office and as soon as I saw the old man he looked like he'd seen a ghost, he said he thought I'd died. Funny that's the same thing Warren said to me in the street. Seems the whole unit had come to the conclusion again that I had died sometime in the past couple of days. My only concern was that probly meant I was not enlisted on the town ledger along with the rest of my unit, the old man said he'd see to it.

Wasn't long before call for us to get to work came in. The city had a pest problem if you know what I mean and we had been selected to deal with it. Just before we left the old man asked me again, "why didn't you die?" I saw you a few days ago, you looked like you were about to die for sure. I seen it enough times to know, I know your tough but nobody's that tough. I spoke the words which came to mind, "I'm not so sure I didn't!"

When we got out there I saw there was two dead deputy's laid on the ground and 1 more dead body, an outlaw's by the looks. Only four of us went out there. The office had to be manned at all times, day and night and two of our unit were taking the first of the mandatory rostered days off. Garcia and Alvarez went round the outside of the ranch so that they could approach from the rear. They had to pass over a decent size hill on the way, they were late to rendezvous with us at the house and I could hear a lot of shots fired so I determined that they ran into a scout or two up there. As for me and Warren we went straight up the middle, no hiding or sneaking up on the house, we just walked up there like men. Guns aimed at the house ready to fire upon the first thing that moved. Just another outlaw posse, Warren started his bullet wound collection with one in the right leg. We finished up and went to find Garcia and Alvarez they were ok, no holes in either of them so we went back to town for a drink. Warren and I had 2 days off coming which we both were looking forward to.

16ᵀᴴ. MADNESS!

Can't say exactly how many times I been shot. How many bullets still remain in me but however many it's quite enough for any man. I guess I'd say I been lucky so far from the perspective that all those bullets hit my body, not one hit me in the head. I been hit both legs, arm and shoulder as well as a few other places but so far not the head and not punctured any vital organs.

That said the last time I was shot almost killed me, don't know what it's like the rest of the world but here some people make their own bullets to save money. In my experience you know if you been shot with a homemade when it's inside you. The last 2 bullets were homemade and not clean I guess that wouldn't have mattered much if I died but if not I would soon take an infection, this is what happened. I could feel bullets tearing roughly through my skin and soft tissue as well as striking and rattling my bones, usual stuff but this time was different to the rest.

Once inside, it started to work on me. Something didn't feel right. At first thought I could not put my finger on it, a nagging feeling but not a desperate situation. The nagging got worse and worse again until it had become more of a desperate situation and then after a few days the desperate situation continued to worsen and the pain and sickness with it, until the point that I could no longer fight it. That was about the time I could not ride my horse. I think I died not long after that but don't know for sure, I can't really remember anything from the time that I arrived at Sagamaw's village to the time that I left there.

These past few months have been hard, I could really use a brief respite for my body to heal and my mind to catch up with the events which have unfolded. I was gonna get a very brief chance to do that. 2 days with no work and I was looking forward to having money. I was to be paid for the first time in my life, I would be able to pay for the things I wanted. From the moment I took those painkillers from the drug store on arriving here in Contention, it was always the plan to go back there this Friday and pay for them along with an apology and a brief explanation. That said, I have been thinking a lot about this of late, apologizing and explaining myself doesn't seem to be at all the right way to go about things. It is the way my mother would have it, that was always a must but this is different. The rest of the world is not like my mother, out here apologizing is like walking around with a sign saying my gun is not loaded. I'm gonna go in there and pay and be sure not to apologize or explain myself.

    I was also thinking about Mimi and the bill she paid for me that time when she cared for me. However much it was, the haberdasher's bill would not have been a lot. The coffee and chicken on the other hand would have been expensive and especially for a whore. Mostly people charge the girls more than the regular price on account of not being able to do anything about it. It ate at me that she cared for me and paid the bill for it from the very modest amount of money she had from that terrible job which I hated her doing and then after all that, I just got up and left! My list was growing what with the drug store and Sgt Green, without a doubt Mimi was top of that list which would be easy. Wait until my minimum term was up then go back there and try to show her how different I was. Try to impress upon her that I was a man now and I could take care of her, if she wanted.

The trouble was gonna be that if I know Mimi she won't have any of it, it would just be an insult to her. She's a proud woman and stubborn too. I knew she hated working as a whore, the things those men used her for and then the things they did to her that she didn't agree to and if they didn't pay, who would care? She would no doubt have chosen to be just about anything else other than a whore, if there was a choice. However much she hated it, the point is she was getting by and she wasn't relying on a man to take care of her.

I'm surprised I understand that and in truth although I respect that about her, I do not like it and I wish that it wasn't the case.

Someday soon I'll go back there and just keep trying to put things right with Mimi and me and I'm just gonna have to accept that is the most I can hope for.

I think that the more I try to change her mind about working as a whore, the more I'm gonna just push her away. If I'm gonna show her that this long year that I been gone has allowed for maturity, then I'm gonna have to accept that she isn't gonna change her mind. I never really thought about the way that others see me, I was always too busy just trying to stay alive. Trying to either avoid or overcome whatever or whoever was trying to claim my life. I guess recently with all this contemplating, I started wondering how people saw me and what the relationship was between the way they thought about me and the way they were towards me.

    Sgt Green for example, why did he give me his old uniform? I guess he was impressed by my joining with the army but it must have been more than that. Maybe he saw in me that I was honest about it and that I genuinely intended to take the soldiering

seriously. A lot of men who were either outlaws or prisoners signed up but never had any intention of being a soldier. I had expressed an interest in soldiering and said as much as I wanted to be good at it and even quoted that I wanted to become a tougher and smarter version of myself. Maybe that earned a small amount of respect with him being a proud Sgt. He kind of alluded to it when he told me that I would earn my place in life and learn the skills that I would need to go through life.
Did I earn Mimi's respect when I stood up to those outlaws in Purgeatory?

    Maybe that is the reason she took me in because she felt like she owed me. I still hope there is more to Mimi's feelings than gratitude but I must put all that aside for now. I can do nothing about it either way until my time soldiering is done and I return to Purgeatory when that may be. I had also to determine what my comrades thought of me, I guess everything happens at its proper time and until now I had no concern about it. I guess initiation was the top priority then getting to our office in Contention. Now that our journey has been completed, I have time to consider such things. I walked back to the army office through town just like all those other mornin's, I can't tell you why but when I got there I had an idea to go round back.

I won't say I sneaked but I was determined to be quiet. I got to the window at the back of the office and I could hear talking. I stood beneath the window and listened to a conversation that took me back to that time when I was just a boy, the last time I was at my father's house.
Garcia had a whole lot to say and the old man was apparently torn between his own feelings on the subject and the so called evidence however compelling presented by Garcia. The subject of this debate was me. Garcia voiced concerns with regards to my mental soundness and listed several key examples that could only be the actions of a crazy man.

I went into Red Sands on my own all guns blazing then turned up half dead 2 or 3 days later. The following day when we were just leaving Red Sands, we headed west to

Contention and we came across that group of men up there at the city limits. I did it again, left formation and ran off guns blazing. One man vs a small posse and I was already half dead from the last time, all pale and weak muttering nonsensical gibberish. Then just recently when we got here and the first job came in, I broke protocol again and elected myself leader. I strung out poor Warren, roped into this idiotic plan of mine to just walk right up there in plain sight and now he's got a bullet in his leg. Meanwhile he and another soldier were dispatched to take out the scout up on the ridge. It's a wonder this kind of stupidness didn't get all four of us killed.

They have all seen it, I died a little while back and however many times before that and nothing is gonna change. I'm gonna get myself killed sooner or later and anyone else unfortunate enough to be along for ride. He then went on to say that he was keen not to be misunderstood. He both fears and respects me and also kinda likes me in a way but make no mistake, I have a kind of sickness that belongs in the wild among beasts and has no place in men.

    I wasn't angry, I didn't feel like he had betrayed me or like I was under attack. Hearing him say it like that I did sound like a crazy man and maybe the fact that none of that had ever occurred to me meant that I was crazy. I agree with his version of accounts but perhaps view them and the reasons I did the things I did differently. I thought maybe if I explained my reasons to them and him in particular they might change the way they see me. Or maybe I felt differently because I was crazy! Then as I hung my head, not in sadness or shame but just reflecting humbly on all that has been said. I pictured me throwing myself around that saloon back in Red Sands shooting it out with a whole posse in a room full of innocent bystanders.

This time of reflecting was gonna be harder than I thought. Truth is I knew that and didn't really want to get anywhere near this stuff, been avoiding it for a while now. I guess it had caught up with me and I was gonna have to face it now, can't run from it anymore.

Thinking back to the time when I was chased out of my father's house all those years ago, I came to the determination that I had to go back there and try to put things right. I was terrified and the decision to go back to the house was hard but actually going back there was even harder. I'm sure that was out of bravery and that at that point I was entirely sane. At some point over these past years had it become less bravery and more insanity? I know there is a thin line between crazy and balls of steel and I know it's hard sometimes to tell whether you're intimidated but defiant and brave or not at all sensitive to any of the emotions you should be feeling and therefore no bravery is required.

That which I think of as defining madness, the complete absence of the emotion or realization that you ought to be feeling at the time given the particular situation. If I was able to do what I do out of madness and no other reason then I would not be able to accept that. I had always thought it was because I was strong and did it out of pride. Thinking about it that day, I honestly couldn't remember the last time I was intimidated, couldn't remember the last time I felt fear. Perhaps I had lost my sanity somewhere back there during any one of those incredible experiences. I was wrong about defining madness, it's clear to me now that madness is simply living without fear. Only with fear comes the impulse to run or to avoid entering into a situation which puts you in danger all together. I did not have that, honestly I feared nothing and still to this day I have no fear! If I am defining madness as no fear then I am forced to come to the conclusion that I have indeed become mad.

    I didn't want my life to be about madness but about strength, bravery and pride.

Now I knew I was gonna have to make some changes in the way I was. Instead of just run in every time there's a gunfight, I'm gonna consult the others, see what they think we should do.

Maybe be better at taking orders and not so keen to impose my own agenda. That might go a long way to make Garcia and others reconsider their estimation of my sanity but I knew that was only a small measure. The problem was that I couldn't imitate fear, I was not afraid of anything certainly not death. Years back, don't know whether I had already lost my fear by then or not, I heard Ed Henry say something, "death only seeks those who seek life!" Although I didn't fully understand it, I knew it to be true. As I contemplated my sanity I remembered that and I knew it to be as true then as it was all those years ago. How can a mad man die, if he neither seeks life nor fears death? How can a man fear death if he is too strong to die?

If a man is too proud and too strong to know fear, how can he truly seek life? I didn't have any answers to these questions and was becoming tired, the life that had become so simple was starting to become far too complicated.

17TH. CONSPIRACY.

I got to the Contention city army office early in the morning the old man already had company, wasn't sure at the time who they were. One man sat at the desk talking to the old man another stood behind him over his right shoulder with his back to the wall. Then two more stood just inside the door, I looked over there but I didn't want to look for long I just stole a quick glance while I was making coffee. The only thing so far I knew about them was they were army too. Hadn't really thought about how long the conversation would continue for or how long they had already been at it but I was curious about the nature of such a secretive conversation.

I was surprised the old man called me over there and was surprised again when I saw who he was talking to, Lieutenant Reid, confederate military officer and director of intelligence gathering for the southern western region. I stood with the old man and listened as the Lt laid it all out step by step, incredible as it was unlikely. A plot to kill every soldier the army put in this office over the past 2 years. He said that was how come he turned up here without prior notice and travelled overnight. He suspects the city mayor's office or the city marshal's office, or both. The only person he is sure is not involved in whatever this was, is the honorable Judge Green, say's he knows Judge Green and that they served together back in '26. He apparently started his investigation over a year ago and so far had worked out that each time the army staff this office, a job comes in to back up the local marshal's office in a raid on a dangerous posse.

    The investigation shows that on each of these occasions the army and deputies go out to the provided coordinates but only the marshal's deputies come back. He said he wanted to flush out the person behind this and he had Judge Green's full support that when the conspirator was identified and brought before the judge he would be tried

and hanged. The Lt said he wanted us to be the ones that expose this conspiracy. He thought that we had the ability and just as important this unit was much larger than the usual occupancy of this office. The old man was a born leader and had greater intellectual capabilities than a soldier usual possesses. There were eight of us in total and he had heard the stories of the half-breed and how tough I was.
He said that's exactly what this army needed real soldiers, tough and smart and fearless.

After he left we called the rest of the unit in to talk about it against the clear specific instructions we had received from Lt Reid. I had a conspiracy theory of my own that maybe this is exactly how it happens over and over again. That maybe the conspirator who sends these men into that ambush is the Lt himself. The old man pointed out that he didn't like the story either but whether we liked it or not it was an order direct from a Lt of the confederate army, our superiors and whether we liked it or not we were gonna have to follow it.

It was to be 3 days from the meeting in the city office, our entire unit was to accompany the city marshal's 11 deputies across the border into Mexico to a town called Las Palmas.
When we arrived there the old man told me, "When it all goes down I want you on the roof."
I told him I didn't like it, I should be down on the ground where I can be effective, he told me he can't make me do anything I don't want to do, everyone knows that. But I said I wanted to try to be part of the team more, show I can take orders too. He wants me on the roof. I can do what he asked me to do or I can do what I want to do, the choice is as always mine. So I went up on the roof, I chose the butcher's shop. The roof had a slight apex and I could use the little shed at the back of the shop to climb up and reach the roof. The location in the street was perfect, I could see all the way down the street on both sides.

When it all started it happened so fast it's hard to remember, I thought about that day a lot since then but I just don't know

what happened. From the moment I heard the first shot, to the moment I passed out went by in what seemed a matter of seconds. The old man was walking slowly up the street in the road, I didn't see or hear anything else before the first shot.
When I heard the shot, I just saw the old man stood perfectly still. He seemed to just stand there for a moment then his legs gave way under him and he just fell to the ground. There was the briefest moment of silence before I saw a couple of my guys run into the street then all hell broke loose. The sound of gunfire interrupting the sound of gunfire, it was like thunder but overlapping and then residual echoes in the distance sounded like it was running away.

They just started dropping down in the street, I didn't know what to do, they all died so fast. The old man, Warren, Garcia all of them dead in the street. I still hadn't fired a shot and I blame myself for that but I couldn't have done anything different, I didn't have a target to fire at. To this day, I still can't remember seeing anyone other than my own men. Without a doubt the hardest thing I have had to come to terms with, and being honest I still haven't, is that as usual I was the only survivor. A nasty habit of mine, not having the common sense to die when everyone else around did.

    I can remember after each one of them was shot down in the dirt, I was standing up on the roof of the butcher's trying desperately to find a target. Like I said the whole thing was over within seconds. All that was left was the smoke filled street and the line of bodies. Then I got hit in the chest, the shot torn my chest open and damn near torn me in half, I fell to my knees.

I heard another shot but I felt it first passed right through my neck from the front to back, I felt it coming in and going out. I was still trying to find a target but my eyes filled up with water and I stopped looking after that. Chest full of shot and a hole through my neck, was dead this time for sure. All I wanted then was to get down there and die alongside my unit, destiny it seems had already made plans.

I was surprised as anyone when I woke the morning of the following day, I felt like shit.
Worse than that, it was like my body was dead but my mind was still trying to convince it otherwise. I came to but I wasn't going anywhere. I wasn't about to get up like I did before, this time I couldn't breathe properly; far be it for me to stand. Seemed like hours of just rolling around on the roof in pain trying to breath, trying to get up. I crawled to the edge of the roof and looked down into the street, their bodies were still there and something had been chewing on em. Coyote's by the looks of, then I worked out why fate would have it that the old man put me up here. If I had been down in the street with the others I would have died but being up here kept me out of the reach of snakes and coyote's. Plus I'm guessing the reason they didn't come finish me off is because somebody would have had to climb up on the roof and they just plain didn't want to.

It took me till near on sundown but I made it down to the ground, would like to say I climbed down but in truth I fell clear off the roof. When I hit the deck I passed out again. I think I must have hit the back of my head when I landed cause I had the worst headache and when I put my hand back there to see, it was covered in blood. My sight and my hearing were pretty much gone to the point that I could make out shapes and slight variations in color but not really see. Same for the hearing, I could hear sounds but didn't know what they were. I know I'm about as tough as they come but if I'm being honest this time I just couldn't shake it.

    I somehow made it to my feet and stumbled the short distance to the saloon, it was pretty empty when I got there except for a young boy who was gathering glasses. I didn't mean to scare anybody, well he got one look at me and pissed down his own leg. I was sorry I scared him but couldn't say so or explain myself I couldn't even speak. He dropped the glasses and just looked at me, he was shaking pretty much all over. I think he was trying to speak but like me couldn't. He did better than I did, I made out two words, "hombre muerto." He ran off after that leaving a trail of piss behind him. I sat at the bar and poured myself a drink. By the time I hit the half way mark on the side of the bottle, I already felt less dead.

Two men came in but not to drink, they came to talk to me. Vincente Almoldovar who I later learned was a (patron)/boss and his Number 1, Pedro Nestor. I said it before, however tough you are. However smart, without luck you're a dead man. Vincente Almoldovar came in to see if it was true. One man had survived the ambush, he stood in front of me as I slowly rose to my feet looked right through me. I mean literally looked all the way through, from the front to the back of my neck and out the other side. He sat at the bar and spoke two words, (hombre muerto)/dead man. I don't know whether it was out of fear, respect or remorse but he sent Pedro outside, not long after he returned with a change of clothes and a girl.

I could barely see her through the haze of pain and alcohol. I just about made out that she had long dark brown hair and ragged clothes. She was instructed to patch me up, in truth I think she was struggling. She ran out a few times at short notice but to her credit both times she came back. She stripped me down to my bare skin then hosed me down with tequila, next she set about stitching me up. I continued with finishing off the rest of the bottle. She got mad cause the tequila was coming back out the hole in my neck and soaking her hands as she was trying to stitch the holes in my chest. The whole time Vincente didn't say a word, he just sat there looking right at me and I looking back at him. When she got done she couldn't get out of there quick enough. I understood and in truth I was grateful but couldn't tell her, I still couldn't speak. After she left Vincente spoke with me a little, "senior, you don't cry out, you don't complain, you really a dead man?" Even if I knew what to say I couldn't say anything, I just stood there and continued to look him in the eye. I put on the clothes that Nestor brought me and then passed out on the floor.

    Two more days went by and when I awoke I saw the boy standing in the door way, as soon as I raised my head he turned and ran. I got as far as my feet then Nestor appeared he gestured to me to go with him then walked off. I made it out of my room and down the stairs. He was stood holding the door open, as I followed him out into the street I saw Vincente and three other men. They began arguing as soon as they saw me about what I can only guess. He spoke to me next, "this man say he shot you in the chest and this man say he shot you right through your neck, what do you say senior?" It was ok that he was taunting me, I wasn't that sensitive and those men did as they claimed.

    I went inside and took the pen from the bar then went back outside. I wrote on my hand, "they must have had their eyes closed!" Vincente and Nestor began laughing, the other men didn't appreciate the humor as much, they walked off just after. First time I had written other than when learning from the old man. Made me reflect on those days and how pointless him and the rest of the unit laying there in the street dead was.

Nestor wanted to buy me a drink and Vincente wanted to talk, he laid it out nice and clear for me. Some day he was gonna finish the job, someday he was gonna kill me but until that day he saw no good reason why we couldn't be friends. I appreciated that honesty so rarely found in men on the so called right side of the law. Seems that only a murderer can be honest of his intention ill or otherwise. We drank a while then he said he wanted me to do something, he said he now knew I was tough but was I trustworthy? I knew what was coming, first I was to get rid of all those bodies in the street then there was a man, one of his men. He was no good, I should make one extra hole in the ground for him. I did it over night while everyone slept, was cooler then and no-one was watching, except Nestor. The man he wanted me to kill was one of the men I met in the street that morning, one of his guys. Hadn't put it all together yet but was getting the sense that Vincente was the person who had done this to me and my unit. The confusion came when he told me two of his men had shot me, so to my mind that was Vincente firmly implicated. But now I had been asked to kill one of those men and was wondering why.

The next day I woke in the room at the Hotel Espirito. Vincente put me in, he said he owned the hotel and I had no place to stay, I would stay with him. I went down stairs and had some coffee that kid was staring at me through the window again. Nestor came in and had a coffee with me, didn't say much, I'm not sure he speaks English. When we were finished he got up and left, I made the assumption I was to go with him and did just that. Vincente was standing with the other man who had claimed to have shot me, "senior, this is Hector, he is worried about his brother Emilio. Do you know where he is?"

Then it came to me nice and clear the two brothers had been working for Vincente who did indeed have nothing to do with the ambush but Hector and his brother must have taken the work freelance. I knew Emilio was dead and was not coming back, I did it myself, put him in the ground late last night. I had pretty strong eye contact with

Hector, I looked down at the ground then I saw he did the same. I scuffed some dirt away with my boot hoping that he would look at my boots and see the soil on them. Then I looked right at him again, he understood what I meant. The expression on his face changed and he began to get angry. Two of Vincente's men were holding him, I tried to gesture that they should let him go, fortunately they must have understood. As soon as they let go of him he pulled his pistol and shot right at me. I drew mine at my own pace and took aim. Being quick is all well and good as long as you make sure you hit something, I'm not sure where he shot but he didn't hit me. I was in no rush, I took my aim and shot him dead. Wasn't sure what would happen next, Vincente bought the drinks and I got the sense I was now employed again.

18‍ᵀᴴ. VINCENTE.

    I had a lot of time to think day after day sitting at the bar with nowhere to be, mostly I thought about the kind of man I was and sometimes I thought about the kind of man I wanted to be. I had a lot to think about but not being able to say anything had changed the way I thought about things. I would no doubt be more economical with words from here on given that I had learned to communicate without words. In doing so I noticed that sometimes an action or even an expression on a face can be a powerful gesture. Counting the sun up and then giving way to the Moon before coming up again the next morning, I reckoned on it being about 3 months now. Not saying that I trusted Vincente or Nestor but I had learned to trust them to be who they were, without pretense.

    I was getting a lot of hate from the rest of Vincente's men. I wrote sometimes on napkins or my hand. I asked him why the rest of his men hated me but Nestor seemed not to, I continue to be surprised by people even after all the experience I had up to that point. Vincente's answer came as a surprise, apparently his men were jealous. Even if I could not talk, I could laugh and that's what I did; wondering what part of me exactly they were jealous of. They were jealous of me for the same reason that Vincente loved me, his words not mine. My genetics, I was born infallible, unbreakable, added to which I am stubborn and unalterable once set upon a target my path cannot be moved. I didn't recoil, hesitate or hide. If I'm gonna be shot, if I'm gonna die. I'm gonna do it with pride, die in style, with dignity!

      He sees most men they turn sideways or they cower. Maybe they hide behind things or shoot from inside a building through the glass so that their target never sees them coming.
Anything to get an edge, to try to avoid getting hurt or killed. I didn't cower, I didn't hide or turn sideways. I stood in plain

sight, faced my enemy and looked him right in the eye, back straight, chest out and chin up. When I eventually die, I was gonna die a gentleman. I would die man's death, not a coward's. Not squeezing off rounds frantically without aim or purpose, shooting behind me over my shoulder as I ran away. A man like me could never die on my knees, could never run away or hide, I would never be able to live with the shame. I would be on my feet when I died and when I got to the afterlife, I would walk on my own feet through the gate. Not be carried like all the other cowboys.

    I'm not gonna lie to you and you probly know me well enough by now, as I sat there listening to him I became emotional. I was determined not to let him, Nestor or anybody else see it. I emptied my glass and set it down on the bar then turned to look at him concentrating hard on not letting a tear come to my eyes. When I looked at Vincente his face was wet, his eyes glazed so that the faint light in the saloon reflected in them. I had no mind to do anything else than just sit and look at him as he did the same. The next few days I did pretty much nothing else other than think about what he had said. As I had done after listening to Garcia that time not so long ago back in Contention, as I recall at that time I was forced to think about the way that others experienced me.

As I thought about Vincente's words, I was once again forced to think about it. I was filled with different emotions. I had no idea anyone thought about me like that. Where Garcia saw crazy, Vincente saw pride and bravery and honor. Naturally I preferred this image of myself to the one Garcia painted. I had to wonder if my persistent defiance of death was somehow gloating, as if to say look at what I do to myself yet my body just takes it. Look at what I can take, what my body can take, look at what they do to me yet my tall, lean, muscular body survives.

My existence is hard, even in a place where life is hard for all. In a time where life is hard for all, for me it is harder yet I survive. Vincente was inspired by the way that I faced all that life had to hit me with, took more than most and yet endured. He was comforted by my continued defiance of death and my refusal of fear, it meant that he too could defy death as he had refused fear. My life was a statement, "yeah life is hard, even impossible and I understand how you feel, I get it. Hard for me too, even harder than it is for you. Yet I don't complain or try to make it easier for myself, I take it head on, all of it. I take it all in a stride and face it like a man with my head up and look it right in the eye and say, fuck you."

    As long as I was still there, still breathing, even though breathing had become so very difficult after the last time I was shot. That meant there was hope for a man like Vincente.

A man in his position would not expect to have a long life. He would not have expected to see his sons as men and had no doubt learned to accept that. But accepting a man's fate was a long way off. There was a new hope that he might be able to change it. Despite this I still expected him to make good on his claim to end my life, I wondered how that would affect him. My life represented hope for him. It represented a world where he could be (el patron) and still live to see his sons grow up. But that was only so whilst I was alive, my death would mean a harsh return to the harsh reality that his worse fear was destined to be his future. This being the man who was sworn to kill me and I expect nothing less from Vincente.

Moving on from that point, I couldn't shake off the feeling that I was somehow different to everyone else, I mean in the way I think. I was only aware how Garcia and Vincente saw me as a person but that information was enough to make me question. It was not just how I saw myself either, for the first time it occurred to me that I saw the world differently. I'm not talking about choosing not to follow everyone else' rules or abide by the law or even just live differently to others. I mean genuinely see things differently. As I said before I knew that I would never be able to understand their laws and rules so I wasn't gonna waste time trying.

By now I was about 18 and I wasn't so sure that not even trying was the right way to go about it. I was still sure that I would never understand the rules of the game but that doesn't mean I shouldn't try. Considering the rest of world judge me by their own standards, from their own perspective. A lot of the time I didn't even know what I did wrong and sometimes I was convinced that I didn't do anything wrong at all. Since it was obvious that I couldn't change the environment I lived in and make everybody else see things from my perspective. I had only 2 choices remaining, either remove myself from the environment entirely or try harder to understand it. I knew it was futile and that I never would understand but that was not really the point. I thought that if others could see that I was trying, they might appreciate that. As I look back now it's clear that despite my ageing, I was still pretty naïve.

    I had decided I was going back across the border to America and so I was gonna have to draw my business with Vincente to an end. If you asked me at the time how did I feel about it, I would no doubt have said something like I felt nothing at all. Now though years past as I look back, I can clearly recall the emotion I was burying and how hard it was for me. I'll be honest now about how I felt at the time, it was horrible. I knew what I had to do and I knew how much I was gonna hate it. Vincente was a threat to America, to the American people and openly had plans to invoke terror upon the American towns and cities nearby. I was an American soldier, preventing terror was my job. It was clear that in my professional capacity it was my duty to remove the threat. The trouble I was having as we rode slowly out of the Las Palmas and wandered into the wilderness is that I was conflicted and Vincente who was in front of me a little and kept turning round periodically and looking right at me was obviously thinking about it too. I dare say he also was conflicted. It was clear to me that there was no way out of it that was the day it was gonna happen.

  We stopped to make camp, we were working pretty well together all three of us. Vincente asked me what I would do if we drew on each other and I killed him. I implied that I'd probly go back to America, what he really wanted to know was if I would take his place as el patron.

I wasn't interested in that, I wanted to know what Nestor would do if we drew on each other.

I used body language to ask him. He was a smart man and he knew what I was asking. Vincente said he wasn't to get involved that it was between him and me; like gentlemen. I trusted that would be exactly how things would play out, Nestor said it didn't really matter either way. If I died they would carry on as before. If Vincente died then he would fight me to be boss and if I didn't want it, he would just take it and my business would be my own. I was less willing to believe that but either way I would have to get past Vincente first. I had never seen Vincente in a draw and had no idea how fast he was. I had to be accurate and fast then be ready straight away for Nestor despite his word. I knew this would be like no other fight, Vincente wanted to die a beautiful death, honorable, dignified and stylish.

We stood no more than just a few feet away from each other, looking each other right in the eye. Nestor just sat by the fire and watched, his body language didn't look like somebody who was about to get up. I could see in his eyes regret and sadness, so much sadness it had always been there. He didn't want to kill me, I knew that and can only hope that he knew how I felt, that I did not want to kill him either. We stood with our body's straight, head up and left hand around our belts. Our right hands down by our gun holsters neither man wanting to be the first to draw. When we did draw it was unspectacular. It never was a draw to see who was the fastest, we both took our time being sure to execute the other man properly out of respect. I wasn't about to shoot that man in the hand or shoulder nor would disgrace this contest by rushing it and aimlessly firing off shot after shot with desperation like a coward. As I said before this was a gentleman's contest and if you were expecting to hear something different then you don't know me at all.

Again out of respect for Vincente, I am not going to go into every little detail and say who hit who and where. Should be sufficient that I'm telling you this story to work out how it ended. I can say that for both of us our need to conduct ourselves properly was greater than our concern for the maintenance of our lives. When I looked at Nestor he was still sitting there just like he said he would do, he too like Vincente was an honorable man as good as his word.

I sat with Vincente for a while, I didn't know why I just wanted. Nestor continued to just sit and drink by the fire, I guess we were wishing farewell to Vincente.

After a while I stood up to leave, Nestor spoke just to tell me he would take care of Vincente's arrangements. That was the first and only thing he said after the gentleman's duel had ended. I took the horse Vincente gifted me after I killed Hector and headed off in the direction of the border. When I was clear of Nestor I stopped for a brief while and turned to look back, I could just about see the fire burning in the distance just then I had one single thought. That is where Vincente lies and he will never leave there and that is because of me. I felt an intense emotion come over me. I am not ashamed to say I wept the whole way back to America not just for Vincente but for the old man too and Warren, Garcia and all of the good brave men who would never go home as I was doing.

19TH. THE MEXICAN.

On the second night I stood up to urinate but did not get that far, instead I had a brief conflict with gravity ending with me falling down right back where I was. I laid there by the fire I had built and looked up into the sky. I don't know if it was me or the world that was spinning but I threw up and shortly after passed out. When I came round it was morning and the fire had gone out, it was at that point just smoking embers. Never a good idea to hang around a smokey fire too long, never know who's gonna see the smoke signals. Problem was that whilst I had the desire to leave, I did not possess the ability to get up off the ground. I no longer had to urinate which I suppose was good but the downside was I had laid there all through the cold night in a wet uniform. When I woke I was shivering. At the time I had no idea what was wrong with me or why I could not get up. I had been feeling so unwell for so long by then, I had gotten used to it.

    I once heard a man say that the sensation of pain is the brain telling you there is something wrong with the body. If that's true then it had been trying to tell me for a while, since Red Sands to be precise which was almost a year ago now. Apparently, I had chosen not to listen. Pain, disorientation, loss of speech and consciousness I could ignore but it's hard to ignore when you can't get up. I got to my knees then I crawled over to the horse. I figured I could use him to hold me up and if I could stay upright long enough I might just be able to get orientated.

    It took a while but I did eventually get up onto the horse. I told him to take it real slow. I was wrong about getting orientated, I felt like I was gonna fall from the horse and almost did many times. He either instinctively knew the way to Contention or he had been there before, cause I was not directing him. Late in the afternoon I saw the town way off in the distance and on the way I had a lot to think about like the conspiracy and who was behind it. Whether to go back to the office or to hide out and a whole bunch of other things.

I had come to a decision on the way, as soon as I get to Contention I'm gonna go find a doctor. I never met one before but I have heard they are real bastards. I just about made it into town, not sure how we got here. We took it nice and slow just like I asked. I rode through the center of town on my way to see the doctor. Everyone just stood there looking at me like that kid back in Las Palmas.

When we stopped I tried to get down off the horse. I don't know what happened, all I know is that I fell on my ass. The assembled crowd, coupled with my clumsy dismount, lead to a slightly more spectacular arrival than I had planned. That was not a good thing, within a few hours everyone in town would know I was back, including the Lt, the city marshal and a dozen deputies. It was destined to be the same old shit all over again, day after day. I crawled into the doctor's office on my knees. Not how I like to introduce myself, it gives others the illusion of superiority.

I told the doctor I could not get to my feet and when I had done previously I fell right back down again. I said the world was spinning and I had been throwing up and passing out.

His immediate reaction was just standing there staring at me and not saying anything. Have no way of knowing whether that was because I had not spoken a word but just wrote down a whole bunch of words and then shoved it in his face. Or some other reason but I had feared that maybe he didn't have the ability to read. Had previously made the assumption that being a doctor he must be able to read. Given that they have to read books to learn their trade, on the other hand it might just be due to my writing. I only learnt to write a while back when the old man tried to teach me and good job he did. Otherwise, I would have no form of communication at all now. That son of a bitch was still just standing there staring at me. I started getting agitated then light headed then I hit the deck again. I was just thinking that this time I was gonna fight it and just then the world got dark and I was out again.

I can't tell you how long I was out but when I woke up I felt numb from head to foot, it was kind of nice there was no pain. Funny it's not until you are without pain for a brief moment that you are able to truly appreciate how much pain you've been in. I just been doing what I always do accept the situation find a way to cope with horrible effects and push on, you do however have to commit a great deal of yourself in order to conjure the fortitude. It's not at all that I was somehow better than everyone else or that my body was somehow infallible, simply that everyone faced with my situation has the option to carry on despite the damage to the body and mind. What most lack is the will to keep committing more and more of oneself in order to keep going, they would be amazed the strength their body has if only their will was not so weak.

The doctor said he put me out with a narcotic then did some work on me, he said he removed the bullets. Naturally I asked him which ones. There was another pause whilst the rusty wheel tried to gather momentum, I imagined I could hear a squeal as it turned. "There's more?" It's difficult when you can't say what you're trying to say, I started to list the ones I could remember by just putting 2 fingers on the area. Don't think he believed me at first, of course once I showed the scars he didn't have much choice in the matter. Only way I can describe it is he seemed to be lecturing me, telling me all about how dangerous it was to leave bullets in the body tissue. There was infections, lead poisoning and all kinds of metal reactions if it was like I said then I would likely not still be alive. I didn't need that bastard to tell me how tough I was or how hard it was for me or even how ill I was. The only thing I needed him to do was fix it. Somehow these doctors had a way of making their trade about something else other than patient care. I knew you gotta stand up to em or you get nothing, just insulted, threatened then accused and finally billed.

I pointed out two obvious but inescapable things. The first is that I was paying so if he wanted the money he had best represent my interest and not his. Second was that I was a soldier, I had a gun and was well accomplished at using it. He agreed to have a dig around and see what he could find. He also agreed to put me out with narcotics again. Which was nice.

By the time I left the doctor's office I couldn't stand being there anymore, he was an asshole. He chose to be a doctor but when it comes to doing the work, he dries up like a leaf in the fall. Kept talking about what was and what was not ethical, damn son of bitch thinks all he has to do is hide behind a big word like ethics. I knew right away what the real reason was he didn't want to do the work because it was too hard and he was too lazy. So he figured he just cook up some bullshit like it's not ethical to inject chemicals into the muscles in my throat every week for the next 3 months. Even though he just got finished telling me that is the only way that he knew of that would ever allow me to regain speech. The muscles in my neck that are needed for speech had been decimated when the bullet ripped through there. I was so frustrated at that moment and not being able to tell him what I thought just made it worse.

I was thinking something along the lines of either you put the needle in my neck or I put it in yours.

There was a trolley, it's like a shelf on wheels. It had a bed pan on it, there was maybe a dozen bullets in the bed pan. Knowing they came out of me made me feel a whole lot better. I know it was just my imagination but I had decided that I felt a little lighter now I wasn't carrying around all that lead! I grabbed a handful of the injections he showed me and left quickly before he started going on about ethics again. What is he a doctor or philosophy lecturer! As frustrated as I was about that militant little man, some degree of balance was restored as I left the doctor's office for the first time in 2 days.

My horse was standing there just like I left him 2 days ago which came as a surprise to me considering all the ways he could have gotten in trouble. He might have wandered off looking for water or food, he could have been stolen. The truth of it was that I didn't know about him, didn't know what he was capable of. Vincente gifted me the horse, at the time he told me the horse had a great spirit no one ever really appreciated but I might. I had noticed the scar on his leg, it was obvious because I have one just like it. The kind of scar which could only have been caused by shooting. Maybe we were more alike than I realized, we both were tough but there was more to it. Often a pack of horses take off when they hear gunfire, there had been shooting since I came by the horse and I had noticed each time that he did not run.

Despite having been shot he was unafraid and when I could not get to my feet and I needed him he could have wandered off and left me there, I would have died there if he did. He knew I was trying to use him to pull myself up, he just braced himself and at one point even lowered his back to offer me a chance. He was smart, strong, tough and loyal we were alike.

There was a young man outside the doctor's office, he said he had been keeping the horse company. He brought him vegetables to eat and clean water. I asked him why he did that, I didn't really get an answer but what he said kind of made some sense. "Mr, this horse… he is The Mexican!" I always assumed he made a mistake and meant to say Mexican instead of The Mexican. I offered the young man some money for the carrots and for caring enough about the horse to do what he did. He said his name was Hector, no relation to the previous mention of the name just a common name among his people at the time.

I knew I was gonna be taking it easy for a few days, taking the pain killers and medicines I took from the doctor. Trying to recover both my strength and speech. Seemed like I was not in much condition to take care of the Mexican. I asked Hector to watch over the Mexican for a few more days and gave him some more money. He said it would be an honor to watch over him. His choice of word got me thinking again, why honor and not pleasure or it would be fine or ok.

I checked into the hotel and didn't give a name at the same time over paying for the room. This in the hope that it would be clear to Mr Brownstone that I wanted discretion.

I took a bottle of bourbon up to the room and used it to sink the painkillers and Echinacea medicine I took from the good doctor. Then I put the first needle into my neck. Fortunately, by the time I injected I was numb again and didn't feel anything, either thanks to the painkillers which were an opioid or the whiskey. I slept like a baby, better than I ever did.

The following morning I asked Hector to explain, did he mean Mexican or The Mexican.

Hector told me a story about a horse in Mexico, its mother died shortly after it was born. The men there at the time thought it had no chance of surviving so they left it for dead. A young boy found the small horse several months later all thin and weak trying to stand but its legs were shaking. The boy

went back there every day for the next 6 months to give the horse water and vegetables he stole from his mother's pantry. One day some men found the boy and the horse and began to bully the young boy. One of the men took out his gun and aimed it at the boy.
The small horse attacked the man and he shot it, it attacked the other men also despite having been shot.

    Over the years many men have tried to claim the horse, many have tried to break the horse's spirit but none ever have. The Mexican has had no master since that boy many years ago, a horse like him can have no master. He cannot be taken as possession or forced to serve, all those who have tried have failed and given up trying to claim the horse. Many have become angry at him and struck out at him. Some have even tried to kill him after being rejected yet still he lives. He requires no-one, if he has need for water he finds water, when he has need for it, he finds food. There are stories of women and boys who have had need for a horse, those few have claimed that he allowed a partnering for short while. Just until they arrived at wherever it was they were heading. Their claims have been mostly rejected, the Mexican has a reputation of being unreasonable, undomesticated and wild. The Mexican is a legend Mr.

Following the story I looked at the horse and perhaps instinctively understood it all had to be true. Knowing what I did about the horse, it was him for sure, the Mexican. Though I knew it was true. I couldn't help notice that he didn't look like a wild, uncivilized beast he just looked like a horse. A few days passed and Hector was true to his word in caring for the Mexican. I had rested and was feeling ready to carry on. I was a little surprised that the horse was still there when I went outside, surprised and happy. I got up on the Mexican for the first time knowing who he was, I had a sense of the spectacular. A sense of being honored to be permitted. But also a sad sense it being temporary, for how long would he allow this partnership. Would I one day awake to find him gone.

20TH. THE LIEUTENANT.

I stood watching the army office from way afar. I had no doubt he knew I was back, they all did. It didn't bother me none, you don't survive what I have endured without a sense of confidence. I was confident that whatever action they took against me, I would be ready for it. I would just shoot them dead in the street and leave them laying there, because that's what they did to my unit. It wouldn't ever be that easy for them again. This time it was me making the plans and them who would be the target. I had that same un-distractible single mindedness as before, I hadn't realized until now but all that trying to fit into the team had made me someone else. I had lost my sharpness and as a result of that fact my team had been exterminated. I had learnt the cost of getting sloppy and would never allow that again. As I stood watching it occurred to me that maybe they knew I was there, maybe they didn't. Either way I was bringing the whole thing to an end.

I wouldn't lose any sleep over the deputies and the city marshal but I had to be sure before I executed the Lt. I didn't like it but I had sworn allegiance to the American army and according to the laws on which it is based, he was still my commanding officer. I saw an opportunity so I took it, he was alone. I walked briskly across the sandy street in the still heat of the afternoon. I knew I was not changing my mind now. I carried a shotgun, not usually my choice. I found them a little unsubtle but on this occasion it was exactly what I needed. The office was the only thing I saw and as I got closer it became the only thing I heard. I was focused and determined with a realistic plan then I heard him laugh out loudly, that was the end of my sensible plan and my pace quickened.

I got to the door I could hear two voices. As soon as I stepped inside I could see one of the deputies standing making coffee. I struck him once with the butt of the shotgun to the head it was a pretty hard strike. He fell to the floor where he stayed for the duration of my meeting with the Lt. I closed the door and locked it, then took the key out of the door and put it in my pocket.

Pointed the shotgun right at him and waited for answers.

"You're angry I can see, you have a right to be."

"All I need from you is did you do this?"

"You're talking, that's a good sign."

"If I just wanted to kill you, I would have."

"So you're giving me a chance?"

"A chance to tell the truth."

"I knew about the set-up, that doesn't mean I did it."

"You knew and you sent my unit to slaughter, you're as guilty as anyone."

"You're not thinking straight! I told you when you came in here I didn't know who was involved, now how else do you think I was gonna find out?" "You are trying to find a justification for your part in this. I'm not in a listening mood" "No hang on, you may recall I told you that you were exactly what this army needed, someone tough, I knew you would survive that's what you do.

I needed to send you in there so you could experience it first hand, then come back here and tell me exactly what happened. Without that there is no proof, there never has been any real proof. How can I call a witness when everyone who goes to that town never comes back? I knew in you I had my opportunity, we are so close now to closing this down for good and stopping these people before they can do it again. I needed you, I still do."

"Well you don't have me, I'm way past working for the army and working for you."

"Wait, don't be foolish you do this for me and for the army and you're done, you have my word. Honorably discharged with a title and I'll pay you severance."

"You can't buy me, I don't want money, I want revenge for my unit."

"Of course you do, how do you think you're gonna get it? Do you even know who to go after?"

"I figure start with you then go from there."

"And where does it end, will there be anyone left when you're done?"

"You tell me who is behind this and I walk away."

"And if I don't?" I figured the best way to answer that was to cock the barrel of the shotgun then aim it right back at him."

"I see!"

If you ask me now a few years on I would say that I regret how things turned out that day. There was an uncomfortable silence for a brief moment then I saw him reach under his desk. I was wound up so tight that I didn't hesitate, I pulled on the trigger and it damn near took his head off"

The noise must have rattled the hive because they started showing up.

First the deputy I knocked out just a while ago, I saw him stir and plugged him twice with my pistol before he had a chance to do it to me. Then three more appeared outside the window that was clearly a job for the shotgun not the pistol, I just had to load it first. The blast took out the window and two of the deputies, I switched to the pistol and shot the last one as he was running off. I only got three of them and I knew there would be more but I didn't yet have enough information and I now needed a new plan.

Thinking about what I learnt from my brief conversation with the Lt, I was interested that he made a point to mention the city marshal several times. Which meant either I was right about the Lt being responsible for this cowardly act and he was trying to implicate the city marshal to take attention off himself. In which case the marshal was innocent of any involvement in this. Or I was wrong about the Lieutenant and he didn't trust the marshal. In which case he was innocent of any involvement and the city marshal was the one responsible.

Whichever one was right, it seemed that my next move was to visit the city marshal's office.

The obvious problem foreseeable was that there was at least another five deputies, all of which I imagined would be up at the city Marshal Office.

It was time to be smart, not time to be brave. The visit to the doctor was a wakeup call. I was pretty tough, about as tough as they come in fact but even then there is only so much a man's body will take. My days of putting my body in the path of every outlaws pistol without so much as a thought for the consequences have to be over and done.

The Lieutenant also mentioned but not implicated the judge, I felt strongly that the judge had no part in this but had to assume the marshal didn't know that. It is possible that if I went up to the courthouse and started shooting the windows out of the place the marshal might fall for it. I was hoping that he would, out of either a sense of duty toward the judge or opportunity to conclude this business with me send a few men up there to take a look. I was keen to find out if he'd go for it but it did occur to me that he might have a couple of deputies up there already. It was risky, I would have to walk right past the marshal's office on my way to the courthouse. If I died there in the street on my way to the courthouse. I would die for a reason and I would die an honorable death, a man's death, a soldier's death and a cowboy's death.

Good enough for me.

As I walked toward the Marshal's Office I could see shadows clambering about the place through the window, I took that to be confirmation that the marshal knew I was coming for him.

I crossed the street and walked along the opposite side of the road by the bank. There was an eerie quietness, not what I wanted, the whole town had cleared inside whatever nearest building.

I made it past the Marshal's Office which told me a lot about the marshal. He must have assumed that if I didn't come looking for him then I hadn't figured him in this conspiracy.

Maybe I wasn't none too smart and figured the judge instead or maybe the Lieutenant was even better than I thought at keeping his cards close to his chest and hadn't given away that he suspected the marshal.

I walked inside expecting to find armed deputies, all I found was a scared and confused judge, a handful of court staff and an old man on trial for sex with a young person not of the proper age.

I put my gun in its holster and approached the judge.

"What are you doing son?"

"The Lieutenant was investigating a conspiracy that had led to the deaths of dozens of army men at the hands of the city marshal and his bastard deputies."

"I know about the good Lieutenant's investigation."

"Yeah well I have taken over the investigation and I believe the Lt was involved also."

"What did you do?"

"The Lieutenant has been removed from his duty, he is no longer in charge."

"This is not right, stop what you are doing."

"I am doing what the army and the Lt himself ordered me to do. I am finding out who is responsible for the deaths of all those men and bringing them to justice."

"Your justice, well that's not justice at all."

"Not my justice, the army's justice. As I would remind you this is the army's concern."

"If you have come to get my approval you should turn around and leave you won't get it."

"I don't require your approval judge, like I said this is the army's business. I just came to see if he had sent any of his men here."

"Who the marshal, you're gonna murder the city marshal?"

"Yes judge I am and his deputies."

"Do you hear the things that you are saying? I cannot allow you to do that!"

"I am sorry judge but you cannot prevent it either, it is my understanding that you control the law enforcement officers in this town, not the army's soldiers."

"No I do not and neither do you, the Lt is the only one who has that authority."

"Finally something we agree upon, I am the Lieutenant."

At that moment I presented the Lieutenant's badge that I had decided to wear for the duration and concluding of this business.

I guess I had smartened up a little in my time soldiering and I had learnt that a brave man makes a fine soldier but a smart man makes a fine officer.

I had read an article in the soldier's legal commitment manual which outlined in some extreme circumstances that a soldier has the legal authority to remove his superior from duty with significant cause. Another which said in some extreme and rare circumstances, a soldier needs a higher authority to carry out his duty. This authority can be claimed by him if there is not a superior officer to award it.

Thanks to the old man for teaching me to read and write, I was able to present this as evidence. I still needed it to be recognized by a person of authority for it to be official.

I was counting on the judge not knowing that and wasn't planning to tell him. He felt like he had no choice but to reluctantly recognize my position as makeshift Lt. I had seen enough to tell me the judge had no hand in these incidents, and explained that the marshal's office was heavily fortified. I figured it better to make a deal with him than defy or deceive him, I promised not to kill the marshal if the judge agreed to help.

The judge would telephone the marshal and tell him I had been apprehended for the murder of Lt Reid. In exchange I would hand over the marshal alive for prosecution which was a big deal. The marshal was a civilian who was wanted by the army. It was common place to be dealt with by the army which the court hated because it meant the city had to accept the lawful execution of a civilian and worst yet, a sworn law enforcement officer. In agreeing to these terms it would also provide the judge with proof of the marshal's guilt. If he and a few deputies come up to the courthouse and arrest me, then he has given no reason to suspect him.

If however he sends half a dozen and does not appear himself he's guilty as charged. The judge could not escape the logical argument combined with my actions being somehow lawful.

Although he agreed to my terms it didn't really matter, I always was gonna kill whoever came up to the courthouse either way. I said before, the people responsible for this don't get away with it but if I could do it all within the law with the judge as witness, then I would.

My gamble paid off, the coward sent four deputies and stayed in his office. I turned to the judge as they walked meaningfully toward the courthouse. The marshal took the bait and played right into my hands. Two men broke off and went to the rear of the building. Suspicion grew on the face of the judge, sometimes you just gotta be lucky. The city marshal was going to be a tough opponent but then made it too easy for me. I walked toward the rear door and placed a heavy desk in front of it. Then to the front I set up to take shots at both men then the unfolding of events lead once again to a surprise.

One of the courthouse security staff was a former deputy and apparently a good honest man. He seemed to be outraged by these actions and wanted a shot at the two men walking up the street toward the courthouse. My luck was in and I wasn't about to question it but I sure found its timing agreeable. We dealt with the two men at the front of the building quickly. Meanwhile, the two men at the rear had tried and failed to get in, instead started shooting through the door and windows. Like I said, played right into my hands. This couldn't have turned out any better, by now the security personnel had started shooting back. The deputies in effect were sieging the courthouse, the judge was now entirely convinced and fully committed.

I left the security to it and made my way to the marshal's office he and one other remained. When I got there I chose to rely on my being in less of a hurry and therefore more accurate.

I did as I said I would and brought the marshal to the courthouse, he was even then arrogant.

The good judge heard his case at short notice and took little time to find him guilty and sentenced him to hang.

CHAPTER 21. IN CONTENTION, IN CONTEMPT.

After the impromptu hanging of the previous city marshal the search began for a new one. Whilst stationed in the town of Contention the marshal was actually employed by Silver City. Like myself and Lt Reid were employed by the American confederate army who were based way out somewhere on the east coast. Each town and city in the west had an army office. It was a deal done entirely at the top, then the order rolled down through the command structure till it got to the governors and council chairmen of each town respectively. It was a similar deal for the city marshal, the deal was done on the east coast. The marshals were employed by the city councils and the judges employed by the town. So in a town like Contention there would be a town judge, a city marshal and an American army Lt. Each had their own office and own staff, apparently each had their own agenda. The army never were friends with the courthouse or city marshal nor the town council more importantly.

After the hanging I began to realize something disturbing, this conspiracy was not thought up at this level. It goes beyond the city marshal and the Lt, but how far up does it go?

This could go all the way up to the top, way out east in New York. If I kept pushing this I would end up in the middle of something way over my head, in a fight I cannot win. I knew this was a big deal and I stumbled right into the middle of it but I was gonna have to keep it to myself. For the rest of my life, I would have to pretend I didn't realize what I almost became part of. I would pretend that I honestly thought I had shut it down back in Contention when that marshal got hung. If I was right, the new marshal is already decided and this open vacancy is just to play along so the public don't get suspicious. It will be announced shortly, the nearest base for the city marshal is Silver City. It will be somebody from there with a name nobody ever heard of. If that happens then I would know I was right about the conspiracy coming from up the top. Meanwhile I had an appointment with the judge, I was told or more like warned not to miss this appointment.

    I was relieved that it was not at the courthouse, I suppose I should be grateful for that.

I got to the motel a little early. I wanted to watch the door, see who was going in. There was a lot of people going in and coming out. Couldn't help but wonder if some of them were there for my meeting with the judge. I went in there walking on hot tin. As soon as I got through the door I was looking around the room for someone reaching for his pistol.

"Relax son, this isn't like the meetings you're used to. I really did come to talk!"

I made my way to the table and took a chair but I was still on edge, he was not alone which was a reassuring sign as it showed he was not entirely comfortable either.

I figured if he was holding all the cards, he would be relaxed knowing what was coming.

He told me to leave his town, get out for good and never come back.

I apparently was the worst kind of outlaw! I actually thought I was doing the right thing that makes a man like me even more dangerous. The kind of man that would never give up on a vendetta, I would hunt a man to the end of the earth just to send him to hell. That town didn't need another undertaker, didn't need a man who would not be put off once he'd made up his mind who was guilty and who needed to be put to death. There already was a system for that, for punishing those people. They got their chance in court to defend themselves and a judge would decide if they were guilty. In some more complicated cases a jury of his peer's would be assembled to pass judgement. If I thought that my style of justice could do better than that, then he didn't want me in that town.

I asked him why he didn't sentence me, hear my case in his court room. He

acknowledged the attempt to act within the confines of the law, that I followed the army's protocol regarding making myself a Lt in order to carry out this task. That I killed my Lt troubled him greatly but as I said it was army business. Had I taken the same action against the marshal, he would have had me arrested but I kept my word and brought him to trial. He thought that I thought that I was trying to obey the law and live an honest life, to make a difference and to bring justice to the world.
"Son, you have no idea how dangerous you are."

    I thought about it a while, couldn't help think about how far up this conspiracy went.
"I've seen men like you before, you think what you're doing is right so therefore everyone else must be wrong, so where does it end?
If I get it wrong are you gonna bring your justice to me?
No one man can elect himself judge and jury over all others, that's why we have this system."

This came at a good time for me, I was already coming around to the conclusion that I had to walk away from this whole conspiracy thing.

"You will realize one day, years from now that you are the one who needs to be stopped. You're not standing up for what's right anymore, now you're just fighting against the people and they're burning images of you out there.

Walk away son before you turn into the people you hunt, leave it to the system".

I know what you're thinking, is he part of this too?"

No, I don't think he has anything to do with it or even knows it exists.

He's just a naïve old fool, he'll learn the truth and next time I won't be there to put my life as collateral against the conspiracy.

I wanted him to know, when I stood up to leave just before I turned to walk out I told him.

"Judge… this conspiracy, you didn't hang it today.

It's not over, not even close.

They'll just send another to replace him and another after that.
You're right it's not my concern, I walk away but you…
You are trapped right in the middle of it now."
He just glared at me, what was encouraging was the look on his face, it was a look as if he was thinking about it.

    I turned and left, not just the motel, it was time for me to leave Contention.
I had been thinking about hanging up my war boots and settling down. My father's house was out there waiting for me and I had hoped so was Mimi. I had thought about her since the last time I saw her years ago. My path was clear to me for the first time in a long time. I was going back to Purgeatory to claim my house and god willing my wife also.

22ND. THEY SAY YOU SHOULD NEVER GO BACK.

As the saying goes, "a lot of water has passed under the bridge."
I had done my time serving as a soldier as well as all the things that come with soldiering.
I would like to say that I was done with getting all shot up and such but truthfully that happened just as much before the army. I had come to the conclusion that the law makers of this great nation were the ones to blame. For their part in allowing whole generations of angry, hate filled and undeveloped young men clearly lacking in empathy, principle or any kind of understanding of the devastation and chaos they cause. To carry modern highly powerful fire arms without any kind evaluation of their mental and emotional capacity.

I would not believe a man who told me, he and his fellow governors did not know or could not foresee that this would be the result. Contention, Purgatory or anywhere else it would be the same, it's important to me to point out that I was not trying to run away from it.

I had other reasons for wanting to go back to Purgeatory, I had been thinking about Mimi and I wanted to see her again. It would be a few day's ride west. I knew a little place with a stream and some cover in the form of a small bunch of trees clumped so close together, it's a wonder how they survive. I camped there and didn't make a fire in case I was being followed.

When the sun came up, I woke as the light had somehow got past the trees and into my eyes. I heard a noise and looked to my right to see the Mexican drinking from the stream.

I took this to be good news, the horse is no fool. If he's drinking it, it must be clean water. That means I can drink it too. As I got to my feet, I looked over at him and I could see him giving me a cold stare. I didn't know whether it was because he was mad at me for something or he was just watching me. I went to fill my canteen with the water for the rest of the journey.

I finally arrived in the god forsaken rat infested outhouse that was Purgeatory. Hadn't changed any to my mind, mostly ignored the looks from all the people stood at the side of the road watching me go by. I tied up the Mexican outside the whorehouse just out of habit. I turned to walk away toward the door before it occurred to me, I did apologize as I untied the rope, he was sure to give a dirty look. Then second time around I turned to walk toward the door, this time I made it all the way inside.

I recognized the old man behind the bar, had forgotten what he looked like but it came back to me when I saw him. I asked about Mimi, I soon wished I hadn't. He was apprehensive and tried to either change the subject and kept asking about where I had been and what it was like or he would try to avoid answering the question. It was really getting to me the way he kept dancing around the subject, was both concerning and

just plain irritating. I stopped him asking questions and slammed my pistol on the bar, I leant towards him and told him like a man.
"I'm gonna plug you right between the eyes if you don't tell me this time, where is Mimi?"
I can see why he didn't want to answer and I was kind of sorry I forced him to but I didn't know.

He started to cry and then I instantly regretted my forthcoming approach. He said that a few weeks back a real nasty group of four or five men came into town. He hadn't seen them before but they were horrid, they didn't have any respect or decency for anything or anyone.
I knew the type, too well. They took what they wanted and they took a liking to her as soon as they got here. I already knew the rest of the story, I'm not sure why I stood there and listened to the rest of it. Out of decency I suppose, he obviously needed to get it out. They took her and a couple other whores one night. She was calling out for help but no-one dared get involved. That

was it, he hadn't seen them or her again since.

As he was unfolding the story I stood looking down at my pistol. From the moment he told me, it was only ever gonna turn out one way. I was disappointed, I had left the army and had started only recently feeling bad about the business of all the people I had killed. Only a few days had passed and as I stood looking down at my gun and my hands I had accepted that I would kill many more men. In this particular situation however, I would not feel bad at all. I was eager to get those men's blood all over my hands. The barman had an idea that they might have been heading north through the native territory. He had heard them talking about all the native women and children they were hoping to kill and rape.

I left in a hurry but when I got outside the Mexican was gone. I took a horse at random from the pack tied outside the forge. Good choice he had been shoed, he was fast too. I took off north as deliberate as I could. Passing on the way what looked like Wolf and Moon who stopped what they were doing to try to identify me. I didn't have time to stop, I found out the following morning that it was indeed them and they set off after me when they made out who I was.

Aside from the whores, they took a few of the young girls from the native village, one of the girls was important to Wolf. She was of course important to all of the native community but especially so to Wolf. It was pleasant to see them both again and I was enjoying the prospect of the three of us hunting together but I had that single mindedness, like a tunnel vision and I was focused on hunting them and nothing else. Wolf said he knew where they would be heading but thought that unless they stopped to have a good time, there would be little chance of us catching up to them now. We fell out several times over the next few days. I wasn't gonna take that as an answer, I was gonna catch up to those bastards if it took the rest of my years to do so.

That was the difference between them and me, between me and everyone else. They thought that we should rest at night

and rest the horses, it angered me. If that girl was important, why didn't they go after her days ago? How come they only left when they saw me leave? They said they almost turned back a few times, they left no more than 5 minutes after I rode by them. I know I was going like hell but they didn't catch up to me until the early hours of the following morning. Not that I slept, I didn't know the territory and wasn't sure which way was north without the sun. I wanted them to come along not least due to Wolf's knowledge of the land, with his help I could travel overnight whilst my prey rested.
I figured if we pushed day and night we would catch them tomorrow, maybe the next day.

    I soon grew tired of their talking and philosophizing and I told them straight. I am going after those men and I will catch up to them. When I find 'em I'm gonna slaughter them being sure to get as much blood on me as possible. If they are not gonna get with the agenda then they should turn around and head back to town where they can sit on their asses and talk. If they stay out here with me then they had better line up and do it now, otherwise I would pull on them myself. I was glad when they finally came to the realization that I was not the boy they knew. They didn't know me at all and it was not too soon when they finally came to their senses.

    We pushed on through the night like I said, it was cooler then so better for the horses. When the daylight came on the second day we came across what was left of last night's camp.

2 dead horses, a burnt out fire and what was left of what once was an 8 year old girl named Geselle. She was one of the girls from the village, whilst Wolf and Moon knelt over her twisted little body and wept I grew quick to anger. I had been imagining we would find something like this and when we did I was not feeling sorrow but anger, so much anger I wanted to kill Wolf and Moon for holding me back before and for crying over her dead body instead of stopping this before it got this far. My hands were shaking, my teeth grinding and

my gaze wide but well focused, the adrenaline filled my head.

    I took off after them hard, I knew they could not be far. I could hear the horse beneath me gasping harder and harder for air in this hot dry and still place. His heart beating so hard I could feel it with my leg as it pressed against his chest. Then in the distance I saw a small dust cloud kicked up by horses. Something came over me, it would be fair to say I was not myself. I was already pushing the horse as hard as I could but when I saw them I tried to push even harder. I couldn't push any harder and neither could he. I think his heart gave out, he cried out and we both fell. I was so close I could see them, then I laid in the dust and watched them ride away beyond sight. I would have given anything for a fresh horse at that moment.

    I walked in their direction for what was left of the day light, in the dusk two riders approached from where I had been. Wolf said he saw the horse a few miles back, I told him I thought the animal's heart had given out. He was not at all surprised. I told him I saw them, not so close that I could hear them but close enough that I could smell them and see the dust cloud they kicked up. Then I watched them ride away.

    I guess I was so focused on the cause of our being out there that I failed to realize Dancing Moon was not the same either. Wolf said he was no longer Dancing Moon, he had become an angry man and would be renamed Howling Moon, the well spirited boy Wolf once knew was no more. I should have been sorrowful about it but in truth I was enjoying hearing all about it that was exactly what I wanted. Wolf said he could go no further, he got down from his horse and passed me the reigns, this business of revenge was for young men.

    I left with Moon and we pushed hard all through the night and in the early hours we finally caught them. We didn't talk much overnight, Moon was fearful and unprepared. He commented that after we have done this we will never be able to go back to who we were again.

I told him I didn't want to hear any more about going back. That who he was allowed this to happen and who he would become will never allow it again. He had lost his young sister to this mob and he had lost his promised to them as well. I could just about feel his hatred and despair, even though my own was all encompassing. I'm not the kind of man to go into every last detail but hopefully it will be sufficient to say, for those of you who are eager for this group to get what is coming to them, they sure did.

    I had seen this kind of tactical plan in the army, being outnumbered ruled out just wading in. There was only two of us but that would be enough to create a cross fire. He would sneak up on them from the front and take out a couple of men if he could, not to kill but to make them helpless. Then when they started to return fire they would all be looking for him, meanwhile I had taken a position from the rear and easily gunned down the rest who were looking the other way. Those who yet lived then turned their attention to me which gave Moon the chance to walk right in there and disarm whoever could still fire a pistol.

I waited till he cleared the camp then came on in there myself. I was drooling over the imminent intimate nature of the following exchange. Those men liked to rape women and children. Having been raped as a child, I did not find it amusing. I took it as my responsibility to remove from each man, that which had been used to rape those poor people. Moon surprisingly was in full agreement which was nice, as were the two remaining whores who had not yet perished.

The two girls were all beaten up and obviously angry. They were not at all put off by the rough treatment those men endured at my and Moon's hands. A man has a kind of peculiar expression on his face when he has had his penis removed! The girls were excited by the opportunity to try a removal using the man's own knife which had a nice kind of irony to it, being the knife he had used to cut them. I figured those men had killed horses as well as women and children. So I suggested a fitting way to put them out of their misery, we laid them close together and had the horses trample them.

I took an inventory of what had been salvaged from this endeavor, well it was not worth it. Geselle the little girl we found a few days ago was Moon's sister. His promised was one of the dead young women in the tent, along with another two young women and three children.
None of them were Mimi. She wasn't here, she wasn't anywhere. We took the two whores and a few horses back to the town and buried the rest out there. I made a wooden cross just like the one I made in initiation. Moon burned some flowers and danced around a fire with the burning flowers singing what he said was a prayer for the dead, to help them find their way to the next life.

We did the best we could by those poor tortured souls but I felt then and still feel now that it wasn't enough. Eventually we got back to town and told the old man who runs the whorehouse what happened and what we discovered. He smiled at the details, they all did.
Moon and I were kind of treated well after that which was nice.

23ᴿᴰ. TO THE MOON AND BACK!

The homecoming was not a thriumph though, as I still had no notion where Mimi was.
I figured if I hadn't found her then she must've escaped them somehow. Maybe she was out there tryin' to get to a town, tryin' to find water. I had to go and search for her. Although I could talk, it took more out of me than I'd care to tell. I needed to rest, I went to the hotel and got a room. I was still taking the injections 'cause, they had to be done each week.

I hadn't stayed in many hotel rooms and this one was like any other I guess. A bed, a dresser with a bowl for washing on it, a mirror and a small shaving blade. It was plenty for me, still found it hard to sleep in a bed, although it felt nicer than the ground, was sometimes too soft! That first night after we got back I was too angry to sleep. I tried laying on the floor and I guess eventually fell asleep there. So I started thinking of a plan to get my father's ranch back off Fitz.

I'd learnt a lot in the army about tactics and ambush. I had the guns I took from those outlaws, so had firepower to do the job. I was workin' out the best night to do it. It had to be right, I didn't want any messing. One evening when I went into the saloon there was a small book on the bar near to my stool. I don't know why but I picked it up and had a look at it. It was something called an 'ol Moore's Almanac, no idea what that was. I turned a couple of pages and saw that it had dates for the coming moon cycles and thought that might come in handy. I had some time before the night I would go to the ranch and decided to spend it looking for Mimi.

The next morning I set off to the wilderness, started off by following the trail Wolf, Moon and I had left when we raced off after those outlaws. I thought about what would be a good way to search for Mimi. In the army we had learned about a zig zag pattern. I thought I would give that a try. I tried to use lone trees and the hills as markers on the way through.

I must've travelled for hours. From sun up, til dusk and so far nothing! She had to be somewhere! I stayed out there overnight and made a small camp on the first night. I was by a small clump of trees near to the opening of a cave. I'd checked it before it had gotten dark and it seemed empty, but I didn't want to be pounced on by something in the night, so wasn't too close. It wouldn't have been a problem to fight it, whatever it was. It's just that I remember my mother saying about the animal world and the animal spirits and I especially didn't want to tangle with one of them if I could avoid it.

    In the cave I found some mushrooms, I picked them up and took them over to where I'd made my camp. I was hungry and as usual didn't have any food, so I thought if I had those mushrooms then that would last me a while. I ate the mushrooms and settled down next to the fire. I started to feel good, it was a strange feeling. I smiled and saw colors jumping around in the fire, they turned into animals and they were smiling at me. I heard music coming from somewhere in the distance, it sounded like the native chanting I had heard before.

    I stood up and started dancing around the fire, then there was a snake dancing with me.
It called my name and we both laughed. The snake said she was called Persephone and she was a snake spirit. We were dancing, I call it dancing. We were smiling and giggling and I could see the colors in the fire jumping around to the music. Time slowed and we danced and laughed for a long time, suddenly I saw what looked like a real snake and told Persephone to stand back out of the way. Silly really as she was a spirit, but I was not thinkin' straight.
I shot at the snake, hard to tell right then if I got it as I could see 3 of 'em. So I shot at all 3!
As the fire died down the images and the music seemed to drift away and I fell into a deep sleep.

    As the sun came up over the ridge I awoke to find a rattle snake shot dead a little ways from the fire and the ground messed up. What was that, was I dreamin' last night. Was I poisoned by the mushrooms? Are there poisonous mushrooms, I didn't know what it was or what to think. I had been riding for a few hours when I saw cart wheel marks with two horses.

I must've not gone this far last time and I could see that the ground around here was softer.

Good, if it's for a distance, I could track this the whole way. Maybe Mimi is on it, where it stopped. I followed the marks for a couple of hours and came across the pram.

There was one man with it and he seemed to be some kind of doctor. In his cart, he had bottles of what looked like medicines. As I approached, he ran towards me and started asking me if I needed help. If I needed help, a strange little man he was. He started talking about his wares. He sold tonics, I didn't know what they were so asked him. He said they were special mixes of herbs and fruits that cured folk. I said "no, I don't need any of that" but wanted to find out which way he'd come from and if he'd somehow seen those outlaws.

Although it occurred to me that if he had, he'd probably be lying on the ground with his horses gone and the cart trashed. I asked him anyway. He said that he'd come from Roscoda. I hadn't been there and thought that might be where Mimi had gone, if she'd escaped them. He thought he might've seen them, it was about a week ago. He was camped overnight when a group of horses loudly rode past in the early hours, they were a fair distance away thankfully. Because now I've said who they were, he was glad they were that far away and his fire had already gone out before he heard them. He said that he didn't know anything else as he'd gone west and kept going until I found him here.

    I thought that as he made tonics, then maybe he'd know about the poisonous mushrooms from last night. He laughed when I told him about it, he said "they ain't poisonous, they're just special. They make you feel good and some folks like taking them." He asked me if I knew the way to the nearest town as he was a bit lost out here. I told him how to get to Purgeatory that is if he could manage to follow what I told him. He set off in the right direction at least! I got back to the zig zag pattern I had been following and carried on heading west. I was running low on water and thought that I might have to go back to town soon. There was nothing around, the land was mostly flat here and in the distance there were small parts with trees. Far to the east was the hills and I was heading there next. I made a camp and decided that in the morning, I would return to town for some food.

      The night went without any problems and when the sun came up, I set off. Didn't seem to take long to get back to town. I went straight to the hotel and then out the back in the outhouse. My mother had always talked about being clean and how that helped the spirits to find you so they can guide or watch over you. So I had always tried to keep myself clean as best I could. Even those years ago in the wilderness when I found a stream I would wash.
I got a fresh horse the next morning and set off out there again, this time was more of an easterly direction, but still heading north.

The terrain started to get rocky as I got nearer to the hills. I wondered if Mimi had escaped near here, that maybe she was hiding out in the hills. I had to check that out so headed on up there. The hills were fully covered in trees and bush. I tied the horse on the edge, just out of sight as I didn't want no-one to steal him. I could've walked back but it would've wasted time and that I didn't want to do. I walked through the trees and tried to keep in one direction but must've got lost. This place was huge and I thought even if she was here, it would take weeks to search it all. Eventually as dusk was falling I found a clearing and made a camp for the night.

Out here by the fire light, laid on the ground looking up at the stars. It was quiet, so quiet that I felt like I was the only one left on the planet. I must've fallen asleep, don't know but the next thing I knew. I was in my father's ranch and mother was in the kitchen cooking. There was the smell of chicken and the fire was crackling and there was smoke billowing towards the door. She was chopping something on the table and threw it into the pot on the fire. Stirring the pot, she looked so peaceful and relaxed. Father walked in and then I watched as we all sat down to eat. I was very small and we were all laughing and talking as we had the meal. I had an overwhelming feeling of loss. The like of which I'd never had, nor understood. It was so real, I could almost touch her. Then she was gone, the kitchen was dark and eerie. Full of cobwebs and a strange smell of rotten food or something! When I woke, I still had that sense of loss. What was it? I shrugged it off as a weird dream and carried on with the task I was doing.

By the time I'd got back to town and back to the hotel room, I'd forgotten all about it.

I still had a while before the night I'd picked to reclaim my old home. Every morning I went back out into the wilderness, each time in a slightly different northerly direction. As I said, I had to follow the sun to help me. So I set off early each morning and if I had to, well I made a fire over night. This was one of those times and yet again, as before it was deathly quiet.

Save for a distant coyote howling which was kind of comforting as I knew it was a long way away and it wouldn't bother me. The fire was crackling and I didn't want it to smoke, but all around the only wood was old and dry. I poured a little water from my canteen on the wood before adding it in the fire. That worked and I settled down next to it looking up at the stars again!

I was in the ranch house and saw my father going to the barn where the bull was. I tried to call out to him, but there was no sound. I ran after him but got there too late and saw him dead on the ground. There it was again, that sense of loss. I'd lost something, didn't know what it was, but the feeling was strong. I woke up to the sound of the coyote howling. It was closer, or was it a different creature. I doused the fire and decided to head back now. The sun would be up soon enough and I had a rough idea of the way until then.

This time that feeling didn't shake off so easily. I still felt weird when I got back to Purgeatory. I didn't know what it was or what I should do about it. It'd been a couple of weeks now since returning to town. For a few days I was just going to the saloon where Moon seemed to have taken residence. I tried to work out what to do to help, but came to the conclusion that he was a man and would deal with it his way, somehow. Moon wasn't in the saloon that night, I took that to be a good sign. Maybe he was starting to sort himself out. The next morning, I looked out of the hotel window. I saw Moon drop down by the wall in front of the whorehouse, drinking! He didn't look none too good. Guess he hadn't sorted it out yet then!

    Honestly, I think it haunted him. He was a deeply spiritual man and according to the customs of his ways what he had done would not be justified under any circumstances. I knew he was struggling with it, he asked me how I deal with it. I didn't know what to say, I had killed countless men and never felt bad. I just told him to drown it until it don't hurt no more, I bought the first few rounds. Upon reflection I regret that being my advice, he never has found an answer at the base of a bottle, yet searches still. Never before have I seen a man so dedicated to the emptying of whiskey bottles. I tried talking to Moon, telling him to get up but he didn't respond. I stood there telling him that he'd had enough time looking at the bottom of a whiskey bottle and now it was time to do something else, he didn't say anything. He didn't even look up at me. He hadn't spoken to anyone since he, well I could say sat, but it was more like dropped down there.

The next day I went and sat next to him with a bottle in my hand and started to drink.
He glanced round at the bottle, not at me. I broke the bottle on the ground as I got up, just in front of him. He didn't flinch. He was much farther gone than I thought. I hadn't realized fully how much had been taken from Moon until I saw him sitting there for so long not moving, except to try to lift another bottle to his lips.

It took me some time to understand why he and Wolf took so long to catch me up while we were hunting those evil men.

They had tried to grieve for Geselle. I had no notion of that.
I'd got hardened to losing people so young and no-one had told me about grief or how to deal with it, so I didn't have any! I was hard on them that day. The dreams I had been getting finally made sense to me and I realized that the sense of loss I had felt after them was grief. Couldn't fix that now, just had to move forward and carry on with the mission.

    I'd thought Moon would come out of it on his own but if he was gonna, it sure was taking some time. He sits barely upright in the dirt against the side of the whorehouse now, from dusk until dawn rolls around. Kind of hard to see him like that, the girls say they can feel his pain when they walk by him. They try to lift his spirit, offer him free ones and such but he just won't get up. Won't even look at them. Some of the other customers complain cause of how he smells. Some say he smells of urine and alcohol. Others say they thought he was dead already on account of him smelling like a corpse, I keep telling myself he will pull through.

The folks saying they thought he was dead 'cause of the smell hadn't been there and seen what I had. Hadn't realized what he lost. After my recent dreams, I was at least understanding it a bit more.

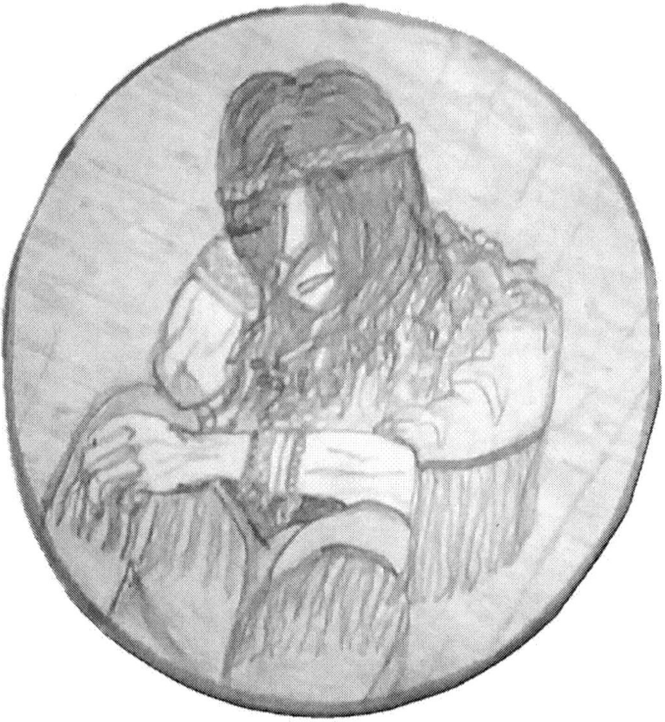

24ᵀᴴ. HOMEWARD BOUND.

Purgeatory is no place for women. It's no place for children or animals or even men of weak nature. There were all kinds here, mostly they were victims, bait or prey. I was one of the few who was not either a victim or a perpetrator, a rare thing here. An angry Wolf confronted me outside the vicarage he was understandably concerned about his son. That was the second day of rain and there was more coming, Wolf wanted me to talk to Moon again to try and reach him. It had been weeks and Moon was still sat there on the ground, even now he wouldn't get up. Wolf first tried ordering me, then tried appealing to me. I was moved by neither. I already knew I had to do something about Moon but he wasn't gonna like what needed to be done.

I had more important things to do, like find Mimi and reclaim my father's ranch.

I would make my move on the ranch this night, had been planning it for a few weeks now.

Would have done it sooner but I have been all over looking for Mimi, looking but not finding.

In some way I felt that she was still alive but didn't know how she could be or where she was.

The whole thing made no sense at all how far could she have gotten on foot, I found the men who took her just 3 days after they left Purgeatory and she was not with them. I been back out there since covered miles of land looking for any sign of her or even sign that someone had been buried like a person sized outline of different colored dirt. I came back with nothing, so I was gonna have to put that on hold for a short while. I had 2 pistols and a spare clip the guns taken from the men I had killed, the new ammunition purchased from the store. There was also a newly acquired shotgun which took a little getting used to but was worth it.

When I got there I stood on the ridge where my folks were buried, I remembered feeling so helpless when I was there last. I smiled when I thought about how far I had come and how I was feeling stood there right then. I had been spending money in town, I also bought a long distance viewing lens like the ones we used to use in the army. Wasn't much help at night unless you could use the moonlight to your advantage, which wasn't always so. Some nights you wouldn't see a damned thing through one of those lenses, I specifically chose this night due to the moonlight. It would illuminate anyone out there as clear as day. I know the land so I knew I could sneak up on 'em from the ridge without making a sound. No moonlight out here so their chances of getting a visual were not good.

The shotgun was for when I get inside, it would be no use to me out here. I had single targets to hit and I had to hit them from far enough away that they would not know I was here.

That was work for a pistol, the outlaw was so loud and so heavy it might expose me, it kind of lit up at the barrel when fired so that would be no good. Still the best thing by far for this type of work was the standard army issue fire arm, had it with me ever since.

I weighed the risks of starting on the left with the fool who thought he was hiding behind the old tree then making my way all the way back across the land to the far right to take the guy on balcony next. That would take too long, by the time I got there I would have lost all initiative. If I start on the balcony there is a chance the fire from inside would pin me down and if the guy from the old tree went the right way, he could flank me then I would be done.

There was only one way for a soldier on his own to do this. I make my way round the outside, round to the left and the guy behind the tree goes first, nice and quiet with my knife. Then approach the house from the rear, go in through that window just like all those years ago.

Open the bedroom door and then switch to the shotgun that ought to wake them up. I opened the bedroom window and climbed in then things got complicated. Fitz had a son in the time I was away, who was now asleep in what used to be my room. I knew if anything happened he would come rushing in here, I baited the trap.

I stood in the corner of the room in the shadow no-one could have seen me there. Now I needed to wake the kid. I kicked the table on the back wall, there was glass lamp on top of the table. The kid woke and sat up, he was clearly startled and afraid. He looked all teary eyed over towards the lamp table. Here we go. I kicked it again and the lamp fell and smashed on the floor. The kid let out a scream and began crying. Right on schedule the footsteps came closer, all the way to the door. Next the door handle, it still squealed after all these years.
The room started to flood with light as the door opened, in walked Fitz.

He approached the weeping kid, when he noticed the child was looking over at the table, he turned his head and looked over toward me. He got the first shot that got everybody's attention. When they came running they saw Fitz lying dead on the ground. The boy crying, staring at his father and the window open. I didn't plan it this way and I couldn't imagine it turning out any better. They ran into the room facing the window with their back to me.

Just one shot left in the shotgun but the outlaw had five, the closest man to me got one shot to the back of his head. The outlaw was in my left hand and the shotgun in my right, the outlaw shot him. The two idiots in the room turned quickly toward me. I discharged the shotgun toward them, it was perfect for that kind of work. At close range you gun down a number of men with just one shot. Down but not out, one man was still able to shoot, I'm not sure what he was aiming at. I dropped the shotgun and switched to my army pistol, just to finish him off. I know there is at least two more out there. The man on the balcony may still be hiding out there waiting for me to think it's clear. First room cleared, I had two choices, make my way into the house or back out the window and round to the front. I went out the window.

When I got round the front, the guy on the balcony was standing no more then 2 foot away from me and no idea I was there. If I could do him with my knife that would give me a great chance of going in through the front door undetected. He was so shaky, even if I got him first I had a feeling he fire anyway. I drew the outlaw on him, it was so loud it was sure to put the fear in 'em. It made a big hole in the back of his head then I kicked the door open and stood in the entrance. Two more in the main reception room, unlike most I learned to shoot with both hands. Two guns, 2 hands that didn't take long then I moved through the rest of the house.
Just one more, a women unarmed and fearing for her life.

I wasn't the kind of man who killed women and children unless I had absolutely no other choice. I told her to take the kid and go but she better not reach for a gun. She ran into the bedroom and fetched the boy. She complained of having nowhere to go.
"Well you can't stay here."

"This is my home, our home."
"No, it's mine and my father's, you took it from an 8 year old boy."
"That was you?"
"Was, now get out, I'm likely to change my mind."
She ran off into the night, I didn't much care where. First job taken care of, now I just had to do something about Moon and hope to hell I find Mimi.

I spent the night burning the bodies then following morning I went into town, Moon wasn't gonna like it but he had it coming. I stood right in front of him and told him to get up.
He refused, I reached down and stood him up. For the record he hit me first, truth is I was kinda counting on it. I hit him back then struck him with the butt of the outlaw, he was out cold. I reached down to pick him up and I was amazed how light he was, his clothes were hanging off him. I carried him on my shoulder to the stable.

I was gonna take a horse but then I saw him standing there, the Mexican I mean.
"You son of a bitch!"

I couldn't help but cuss him, even though I knew why he did it. Somehow he knew that I was going hard into the night and whatever horse I was on wouldn't be coming back. I threw Moon over the Mexican's back and walked off, he'll follow when he's ready. I walked back to the house. Each time I turned to look back, the Mexican was getting closer and closer. We got back to the house around midday by the looks of the sun in the sky and the shadows on the ground around the house.

    An unexpected kindness was that I did not have to do any cleaning up. I guess on the account of Fitz having a woman here and her kid lived here, it not a surprise that she kept this place pretty much pristine. Apart from the newly spilled blood, but that wouldn't take long to clean up. Was trying to think back to the last time I was here and how long since my mother was here, she kept this house with pride. She was the kind of woman I hope one day I would find and she would come keep this house just like my mother did.

I put Moon in what used to be my room, laid him on top of the bed, he sure did stink.
Went outside to have it out with the Mexican, damn bastard. I got there and stood on the porch, he was looking right at me. So I told him like a man, "you're a damn bastard you know that."
He turned and walked away, I guess that's it for now. Moon will be out for a good while yet and the Mexican will just go do his own thing. I decided I was gonna sit out here on the deck and drink my coffee, then take a walk into town. I felt like things were looking up for me.

That was the first coffee I had in I cannot remember how long, I have Fitz to thank for the coffee. I walked along into town like I did that first time when I was just a boy. I am entirely unashamed to announce that I smiled all the way. I had a spring in my step that day, I did my time in the army, getting shot up, starving, dying. Now I'm a man, my own man. I got my father's ranch back, I didn't owe anybody anything. Now I needed to see about some form of making money. I never really been employed before and I was unsure about what I would have to do. I still had little money from before but I was looking for something long term, for the future. That and also I was looking for Mimi.

25TH. OLD MAN NOLAN.

So just as summer came around the ranch was full of life, what with Moon living there and two sisters we met at the saloon. Clancy and Maria had moved in sometime over the past couple of weeks. I'm still not really sure where they kept themselves, maybe in what used to be my mother's room. It would make sense given that it had a vanity unit and it used to be a woman's room. I don't know it's a big house, I know that at night I could hear talking and laughing and arguing but mostly arguing.

It made the house feel full of life. I remember when this was my father's house, it was big and quiet and empty and cold. He had a kind of unspoken rule, he would set the fire at 4 oclock in the winter and around 7 oclock in the spring and fall. The two sisters who had moved in quite without invitation or even without my knowing, had decided the fire should be on all day from around noon till dusk.

There was no funny business between me and the sisters, I can't speak of Moon's comings and goings but it did seem unlikely given the condition he was in. I guess I kept them around because it made the house feel warm, there was also a pot of coffee in the kitchen any time of day. The house would be warm and light and there was always conversation or laughter. They kept themselves mostly to the third floor where my mother's room was.
It was nice having them around and really it was the complete opposite to the way I remember it growing up.

Clancy was the more talkative of the two. I encountered her in the kitchen one day, she introduced herself as the clever one. I mentioned that the money was running out and I was looking for something profitable to get involved in. She told me about a man she used to endure, he boasted of the money he made rounding up outlaws and bringing them to court.

An outlaw was a man who was wanted by the law, but the law either didn't know where to find him or couldn't bring him in. Would pay well for any man who brought these criminals to the law house.

That day I was going to see the city marshal about six men he wanted. He put an unusually large bounty on the men, I knew who and where they were. I asked Clancy what she expected in return, she was content not to be knocked around day by day. That was a done deal as far as I was concerned.

So yesterday I was a poor land owner with no profit and today I begin a new life as a bounty hunter. I knew from my time in the military that I would take to this new business like a baby takes to crying. When I arrived at the new city marshal's office the following day, I met the man who held the money. I didn't know it at the time but I would come to regard the old man as one of the few people I really liked. Graeme, he said his name was.

I found him to be an impressive individual. Being a person who never took a liking to anyone, it was an unusual experience for me to genuinely like someone.

He was the kind of old guy who had been there and seen it all before, he knew what the young men where all about because he used to be one of them. I felt like he didn't need a man to share his ideals in order to accept him as a man. Not to say that he agreed with everything I said or believed, he made it clear he didn't but there was no animosity. He would tell a man what he thought of him one minute but the next it was forgotten.

I recall a time I was working on the farm he came to see me, he was talking about a horse he once had. I was concentrating on what I was doing and I had not been listening, he kicked my leg and called me an ignorant bastard. I was not offended but instead apologetic, he had a way of being brutally honest but without causing offense. I was impressed by him and I think he in some ways was impressed by me. I took from there a signed letter naming Ely and Josephus James, Dean

Samsson, Arvide O'connor, James Maccarthy and Guy Nelson.
It took me 3 days to return with all six men. City marshal Nolan awarded almost 1000 dollars, I was a wealthy man. I continued to work for Mr Nolan for a further 8 months until one day he just wasn't there anymore.

He had been a deputy and then a sheriff in a long and successful career as a lawman.
He had retired from the law keeping business aged 75 due to severe lack of interest. He had been persuaded to take the office of the city marshal after a young law man had removed the previous one for treason. That young law man of course would be me. He was nothing like the previous and removed city marshal. I was sad when I learned that he had passed away one night, but pleased he passed in his sleep. I went to the saloon to celebrate him and my new fortune.
"To the old man."

Seems the good ones are gone and the world is left to the idiots.

I choose to carry on the law keeping business in the way that old man Nolan like it to be done.

Maybe one day I'll be an old man talking to a young man who reminds me a bit of myself when I was his age, and I'll tell a story of a likeable old man I once knew when I was young. I can only hope of course that I would be as likeable and intriguing when I am old as old man Nolan. I just kept thinking about him, he died alone. I will regret all my years that I was not there to see him off. I wanted to be but I was afraid I would impose as I was not family. So long old man. As for me, I was proud to be the new city marshal.

26TH. CHAPTER. THE NEW MARSHAL.

So there was a fair bit of resistance to my being named city marshal.

I am no fool, I know this is not a permanent appointment. It did make a lot of sense being on good terms with the old man and I was the person who removed the previous marshal. I was of the opinion that even marshal Nolan's appointment was temporary. I don't know who they were waiting for but they hadn't found it yet. I was asked to hire a team three to four men, I had pretty much put the team together as soon as they asked. Well, in my head at least.

It would be myself and Moon no doubt, then I wanted more military experience. Sgt Green the massive man who handed me his uniform all those years ago when I went to initiation. Dean who was a man a little older than me and worked for a short while in Silver City as a peacekeeper for the rail road. I saw him as an honorable man, the railroad had a habit of hiring men to protect it but without realizing they hired men from within the gangs that robbed the trains. Rather obviously their peacekeepers didn't do very well and didn't last very long. Dean had been a railroad peacekeeper for almost 2 years meaning two things. He was obviously trustworthy and given 2 years is an extraordinary long time for a man in that work. He was also obviously good at the gun work.

I would need one more, I knew I wouldn't be city marshal for long but maybe when my time in that office comes to an end the city will keep the team at least that was my hope.

I thought that if I put the right person into the existing team then the city might hire him to replace me and therefore keep them intact. The difficult task ahead for me now is finding that person. There is no chance of them appointing Moon for two good reasons. One, he has no real experience and two he is a native. Sgt Green should have been in the running for that position long ago but he had an equally poor chance of being marshal for 1 reason alone, he's black.

Dean had a great chance given that he had worked for a city before, having kept the peace in a big city like Silver City. Two years of gun work in a city like that made him more than qualified for the gun work in Purgatory. As a marshal though? I do not know. Dean had something else going in his favor, he was their favorite color. With all this goin' around my head, it's a wonder that I had time to think about Mimi.

I had pretty much accepted that I would not ever see her again and it's likely she's dead.
Even though I knew all that, I just still kept thinking of her. I dreamed at night that I found her.
Different dreams each time, sometimes she's standing in front of me looking just as beautiful as she ever did, in a torn white dress with a red lace scarf. Other dreams I have I find her dead, her body and face all bloody. The stink of decay is unpalatable to all except the flies buzzing round her and the damn wolf chewing at her leg. I think I prefer not knowing for sure, not having proof either way. This way there will always be a little part of me that thinks she somehow broke away from those bastards then some honest cowboy came across her and put her on his horse. They wed recently and she now bares a child. I like to think that but I don't really believe it.

Back to the task at hand. I arrive at the office of the city marshal to meet with delegates of the township. I remember the enthusiasm they couldn't hide, I had a long exchange with them about their plans and their hopes for the town. Two hours later they started talking about the subject that brought us all there, it would be fair to say that I had not been so enthusiastic.

We finally got around to the proposals for the team, I went with Dean first. They loved him and I got unanimous invitation to hire him. Following their approval of Dean's history of gunwork, I thought that was as good a time as any to propose Sgt Green. Their enthusiasm ended quickly, I was however prepared for that and employed a little politics.
A fine argument well put together just about swayed them but I had hoped for more enthusiasm for a man who had been a Sgt and had an exemplary record. A man who had already lead a team with a gun in his hand.

Moon was always gonna be tough to sell but I knew how I was gonna propose him. We need a native to talk to natives, I knew they would agree with that so I proposed him as a translator. That did it but only just, now I had a team but I needed one more. Someone who would honor the team. I wanted to head home but first I stopped to speak a little with Sgt Green, my impression is that he was happy to have work although he was unconvinced he would be paid. I assured him that they were just as likely to not pay me but in the event of that happening I would lock up the office and allow a justice holiday for the town until the fault was rectified. I could tell he didn't really want to do gunwork but he wanted to feed his family, I know that is a pretty strong motivation.

    Dean was an enthusiastic individual and I was assured a typically keen response, he was relieved to have employment again after quitting his job with the railroad. The kind of work didn't seem to bother him, he was younger than the Sgt and I am just supposing that when he is a similar age he too will despise the business of killing for remuneration. If I am to be honest with you, I already did and have for a good while now but I do realize that it never used to bother me.

I got back to the ranch and was met with another of life's surprises. I don't know how else to describe it other than merrymaking. Moon and the two sisters were dancing and singing, well that's misleading. The sisters were dancing, Clancy was singing, Moon was kind of just standing with them but he was trying to join in and smiling. Here was a man that couldn't get up off the floor just a short while ago and now here at the house, smiling. They had music playing and all the windows and doors wide open. It was a nice hot day by the smell in the air summer had come. Moon had been having some tough times and it all really got too much for him, he deserved a little happiness. Although they didn't talk about it much, I knew the sisters had really been through it. Like I said towns like this are no place for a woman, they had no rights.

But here at my father's old house as I stood on the porch and watched them, they looked like for the first time in their lives they felt free from it. I was pleased for them and was glad that the old place had a use again, I think I even smiled. That didn't last long when I realized it would only be a matter of time before one of them saw me standing out here and dragged me into it, I was terrified. I had never danced before, I would be stiff like a board and I had little to no idea what to do. I took my chance to bail out but I kept the smile they gave me. I turned and walked to the rocking chair and sat for a while on the porch and just watched the sun set on another wild day in Purgeatory. You truly do not know what the next day has lined up for you or the one after that, as far as days go this was a good one.

    Clancy came outside, I had been discovered but it was not as bad as I had initially thought. She brought whiskey out from the house with 2 glasses, I had no idea we had glasses or whiskey. She sat with me a while on my lap and we watched the sun disappear behind the big rock up on the ridge. I was enjoying that moment but I could not sit there without thinking about my mother and father. It felt a little like, in a way some part of them was still here.

I wondered what they would think of all this, I think they would approve.

We sat pretty much in silence, her head rested on my chest and shoulder with her glass in one hand and the bottle in the other. Whenever my glass was empty, she would just pour a little more in. She didn't talk much that whole time, I didn't push her to. It suited me and I figured if she wanted to she wouldn't need invitation. After dark she got cold and went back in the house, we said good night and I thought no more of it. I stayed up a while longer then took what was left of the bottle, said goodnight to my mother and father then went to bed.

Well, life is just full of surprises is it not?

Clancy said she was going to bed but she did not say whose bed! So for now at least, for the four of us things were well. And thanks to Clancy and the whiskey, for the first time in a good long while I was not thinking about bounty hunting and marshalling or soldiering, death and dying or Mimi. No doubt come tomorrow I sure would be again but at least for one night my head was clear of it all.

CHAPTER 27. DISCOVERING SENIOR DELGADO.

I was still looking for the all-important 4th member of the team, the final member.
In the meantime we had started a new era in Purgatory for the first time native, black, Latino and white all had a voice. Most of the work was breaking up fights, disputes over land or livestock and from time to time a posse of merciless outlaws would hit town. I was asked to investigate two missing men, they were cattle steers. The team leader was an old man called Laurens, they had been investigating missing cattle. I had developed a sense of irony.

Laurens was a soldier himself but that ended around 35 years ago, he served 2 times.
The first a 3 years service that saw him travel south to Mexico and Ecuador. The second service also 3 years, less travel

however. He was stationed in Silver City for the most part of the second service. In that time two of his nearest and dearest were killed, the first was his young wife Matild. They had only been married 4 hours, he said they had not consummated the marriage. Shortly after, his second had been killed during a rather routine fight break up. He quit not long after due to ill health, not sure what the diagnosis was.

In the time that he had been retired the law had not changed, the criminal mind however had. It's always difficult to deal with the public in these situations, you could try to imagine what it would be like when the member of public is a former city law man. Anyway he had reported two men lost somewhere in the foot hills, apparently they were there one moment and gone the next. I had to investigate whether I wanted to or not. The trouble was the only information I had to work with was his account, which made no sense at all.

He was respected by the members of the city council, so any idea of dismissing the old man's case would only result more questions and issues. I sent the good Sgt, Moon and Dean to investigate. It didn't make a whole lot of sense to them either, the report they handed in was based on the idea that two people and 2 horses just disappeared. We followed every lead and had nothing that made any sense. Towards the end I was getting agitated, I asked Moon's father Wolf to follow the tracks. It took him only a couple of hours to ride out to the foothills, follow the tracks, and search the area for any other clues and return to give his report to me.

Wolf said that there was only ever 1 set of horse shoe tracks, I respected his opinion as I knew he was a master tracker. That gave me a difficult situation, I had no choice but to challenge either the old man or Wolf.
I can honestly say I didn't feel comfortable challenging either one, the case however had to be finalized. Responsibility, sounds great until you have it.

Dawn broke the second day of the investigation, after coming up empty with the native high chief and the standard investigation I was beginning to worry. I didn't want a case that I didn't understand to go on and on, besides any man in my position wants to get the first few cases satisfied as soon as possible. I rode out there myself, it was the middle of the night and I was alone. Best for thinking about issues that I didn't understand, nothing like peace and quiet to focus the mind.

I had military training, I was as likely as any man to find the answer and this story had been told in town. It had gathered quite a following, the local news journal had decided on a 3 page center piece. While I was out there I looked and looked again but I could not find any evidence of the two missing men or their horses. I was stood right where the two men had been when they disappeared, yet there was nothing. In the cold dark night I mounted the Mexican and headed back to town, I unlocked the town marshal office to file my report.

I was alleging that the old man had ridden out there by himself. I know, confusing but I had to be honest about what I had found. I surmised that the old man had been a victim of a trick of the mind, he had conjured images of two deceased fellow steers. In his grief, he had genuinely believed them to be real. He had experienced a brief and unexpected moment of clarity during which he had realized the two men he had claimed to be riding with, did not really exist. The problem with this is that the city had been paying him and his two compatriots for the past year or so. As I asked around I could not find anybody who had met these two men, yet the city had continued to pay them. How then was I going to tell the city council members they had been paying two imaginary men!

    I had no interest in being their friend and had already decided to just tell them as it is.

My way, you ask anyone in town and they'll tell you. I am an asshole, rude, arrogant and ignorant. I am stubborn and set firmly in my primitive ways but honest and transparent. For those who could appreciate that, just about tolerable. For others, I embodied all the things they're comfortable belief system programmed them to both fear and hate. Ideal credentials for a city marshal.

The problem I had was that the relentless outlaws of Purgatory didn't recognize my superiority, coupled with the obvious issue of being a half-breed. Having the reputation I had apparently gained over the past years, has only inspired those who would seek glory to be even more motivated to challenge my team, the city and more specifically me.   Which generally left me with only one choice, nondescript gratuitous brutality. I didn't have many prisoners. I had an idea that the right character might inspire more cooperation among the worst of the west. As I have said before the universe, quite unexpectedly provides sometimes. Senior Delgado. Remember that name.

CHAPTER 28. BETTER THAN THE ONLY REMAINING ALTERNATIVE.

Midweek early afternoons were generally a pretty quiet time.
Just across the street from my office there was a disturbance, a man was accused of shooting another man's horse. When the perpetrator was confronted by the horse owner, he became violent and shot the owner. I was tasked with arresting the stranger for prosecution, shouldn't take long pretty straight forward. I took a slow walk over to the saloon. The perpetrator was in my sights, he turned to head inside. Only moments later I followed him into the saloon, he was sat on the floor cradling a dog. The dog was his and the other man lying dead in the street had allegedly shot the animal. He understandably took it poorly.

The law specifically prohibited an eye for an eye, personally I thought his response was justified but professionally I could not approve. According to the law, my response was required. Personally I thought it was justified however he could not approve. We had a kind of standoff I informed him I was a law man, he said so was he. I figured wherever he was employed as law man had a very different concept of law.

I had noticed when most people point a gun at me it's no more than that, just a threat.
This time however was more than a threat, his hand was as still as my own in that situation.
In my experience most people just point and squeeze I however never fired without aiming at something, heart or forehead. His head was tilted to the right and one eye was following the barrel of his gun, he was a killer no doubt about it. I knew he didn't lose these standoffs because he was like me and I didn't lose these standoffs either. There was no need to talk trash, usually in these situations there's a story about how

dangerous the other man is. I didn't go in for the threats and self-made legends much, as we stood there in silence looking at each other, I kind of respected his non bullshitting way.

    I always figured if a man is truly as tough as he thinks he is, he doesn't feel the need to prove it or to tell everyone else. I been in enough of these situations to know how this turns out, we fill each other's broken bodies with bullets and see who the toughest is. One man walks away and adds another chapter to his ever increasing legend, the other lays in the dirt for a few days attracting flies until the wild dogs drag it off into the desert. Don't misunderstand me, I back myself in all such circumstances and this one was no different, it's just that I had learnt from a previous experience back in Mexico. Either myself or Vincente was gonna die and the other had to continue killing for years to come. I remember I didn't much fancy either outcome but someone had to live and someone had to die. As it was he died and I still think about him from time to time as I do all the men I have killed. Most of them deserved it and I didn't feel the least bit bad about it but when I thought about Vincente I felt terrible. I respected and admired the man and didn't want him to die but when it's me or him, I only had one choice.

I thought many times what could I have done differently, how could I have avoided that situation?

This time I was gonna do it differently, I kept my eyes focused on his, but slowly lowered my pistol. I put my hand behind my back and tucked the gun into my belt, pulled my shirt over it and stood with my hands by my side.

"What are you doing senior?"

"I'm having a drink!"

I walked to the bar and sat at a stool with my back to the man. Earn, the owner of the bar seemed perplexed by the event, I ordered a cold beer and sat in silence. I was hoping senior Delgado would sit and drink with me so that I would not have to kill him. I'll be honest with you as I always am, I was relieved when he sat at the bar beside me.

"You got balls senior."

"What will it be?"
"Whiskey!"
"You heard the man Earn!"
Earn served Delgado a whiskey and the room slowly began to move again. Fascinating thing I can't explain it but sometimes you can actually feel the tension disappearing. The bystanders previously frozen in time, now slowly reanimating.

We sat for a while can't say how long, sometimes I get caught up in the moment, think with my heart and not my head. I usually regret such times and I knew this was one such occasion but was compelled, faced with the alternative, killing the man. I had a few points in mind and such is my way, I just come out with them.
"What was his name?"
"I don't know what you are talking about"
"Your dog, what was his name?"
"Caesar!"
"You should bury him."

He didn't respond and we didn't look at each other. Earn stood in the corner of the bar at the far end polishing glasses, just looking at us and absorbing every word exchanged. As for Delgado, he sat quietly drinking his whiskey and more importantly not being an outlaw gunman. I finished my beer and stood up, put my hat on and thanked Earn.

"I gotta deal with the body you left in the street."

I put a dollar on the bar knowing that would cover mine and his drinks. As I was walking out I left an instruction, unsure whether he would follow it or not.

"Come and see me at my office when you get done with Caesar!"

When I got back to my office, I rather expectedly came under fire from some of the towns more influential citizens with regards to my handling of the Delgado situation. I repeatedly assured them that I had in fact dealt with it and I had a plan that would benefit more than just the town's undertaker. He unsurprisingly had become one of the wealthiest men in Purgatory. I made arrangements to dispose of the body in the street and to bury his horse.

Although, there was some feeling among the council chairs that should have been the other way round.

    Around 16:00 senior Delgado walked into my office, when I saw him I wanted to smile but I just about managed to contain it. If I could have scripted the situation, I would have told him to sit down and ask me why I wanted to see him. To my amusement he sat and asked me why I wanted to see him. I felt at that time that my plan was the right thing to do.

"You said you were a law man?"

"Si senior."

"In Mexico?"

"Was."

"Was?"

"Mexico is my home but it is a poor land and America is the land of opportunity."

"Opportunity, is that what brings you here?"

"That's what I said."

"Well, I have one for you."

"You have an opportunity for me?"

"Law man, that's what you do isn't it?"

"You want to hire me senior?"

I sat back in my chair, put my feet up on the desk and took off my hat.
"Well, I would prefer that to the only other alternative."
"Which is what?"
I didn't reply, I leant forward put my hat on the desk and then sat back and just looked him in the eye. The sun was high and when it comes in through the window it hits me right in the face, I couldn't help but narrow my eyes a little.
"I see."
"Well, what do you say?"
"Si."

CHAPTER 29. WAITING FOR A WOLF.

   Senior Delgado seemed pretty eager to join the team, a thing I was both relieved and excited about. It also kept the town council off my back about completing the team. I'm sure you won't be surprised they didn't like my pick, it's not the first time for that. Sometimes small talk can be hard, the period of getting to know your new colleague is a difficult one. In this case he found it hard to talk to me and the rest of the team, I don't suppose that's too much of a problem except I got the feeling there was something he wanted to say.
   A few weeks went by until one fine evening, myself and senior Delgado spent the night watching over a man and his wife who were expecting company in the form of a mob.
I didn't go much for the intimidation and bullying tactics but I have to say the man we were protecting was without even the most

basic fortitude. Laid outside under the stars that night by the fire, nobody came but Delgado mentioned a name I had not heard for a long time.

Do you remember that little town in Mexico, was a slaughter.
A good friend of mine (Vincente) died and I got shot, a bullet passed right through my throat.
Other men remarked that they could see daylight through my neck. The only man as far as I can recall who didn't get shot was Vincente's number 1, Nestor. Senior Delgado mentioned Nestor. I wasn't sure what to think. The story as far as I know it is that Nestor has been talking about (el hombre muerto), as he used to call me. Delgado had come from south of Mexico and upon meeting with Nestor been interested by the story of the dead man. Nestor had told him that the dead man had gone back to America, Purgeatory he thought.

It's worth mentioning, I think that Nestor had a small fortune offered against the death of el hombre muerto, me. I wasn't bothered by this confession, rather comforted by it. I knew there was a reason for Delgado being here, as long as he was hiding it I felt I could not trust him or rely on him. Now he had come out with it, I felt that we were building a relationship based on truth. This information made me feel like trusting him; that said I also knew that this meant we would have to end our friendship at some point in the near future.

The question now becomes, does this effect his ability to do his job and if so how does it.

I had hoped that he would be professional enough to compartmentalize the work and our personal affairs. Delgado was good enough to point out that he didn't want to kill me because he had a dislike for me. He wanted to kill me but it was because the legend of el hombre muerto. He was one of those people, I didn't hold that against him, instead I appreciated his honesty. In my mind to be honest with a man meant respect, to share information that could be dangerous with your intended target means two things. Firstly, that you think he deserves to know and secondly, perhaps more importantly that you trust him not to change, having been provided with said information.

For a man to remain unchanged by the information that attempts will be made to end his life is unusual and impressive. So I had learnt that Delgado as part of the team would not be long term, this presents two problems for me. One is that I would have to find another to replace him and the second is that at some point either he will kill me or I will have to kill him. Which of course is what I had been trying to avoid. It reminded me that the life of a city marshal was much the same as the life of a gunman. I wanted free of that and I already wanted free of the position of marshal. Still I felt that my leaving would depend on my ability to find a replacement leader. Whoever he was he seemed to be eluding me which was becoming a rather predictable source of frustration.

I respected Delgado enough to depend on him finishing this assignment with me before any personal business got in the way. The sun rose the following morning, as we packed up our things I wanted to initiate dialogue with regards to the subject hanging over us.

"How much is the reward?"

I didn't need to be looking at him to know what the reaction was. I continued packing my things on the Mexican, Delgado didn't answer that particular question but did say that he didn't want to get involved in that yet. There was plenty time for us to get to our personal business, this was the time to work.

    I spent the entire summer waiting for that particular time, he would visit the house often and a few times a week we sat at the bar together. Moon insisted it was a mistake to bring him to the house and that I was trusting him too much. Stating that Delgado was a bounty hunter and he had already confessed that he wanted to collect on me. I wasn't worried about it, I trusted him to keep his personal business separate and I wasn't the kind of person who played silly games with people so I would give Delgado no reason to do anything unfriendly. Well even if he did try something and I was wrong about his character, I still wasn't concerned because I knew what ever happened I would deal with it. Moon was a worrier, it was in his nature. He didn't seem at all reassured by my dismissal of the subject.

The following day he returned to the house after visiting his people at their village, just the other side of the mountains. He was asked to pass on a message to me from his father.

When I saw the wolf, I was to visit him at the native village. Your guess is as good as mine, like most of the messages from the spirit world, it was unclear what it really meant. The idea as far as I know was, that the message was supposed to be unclear until the moment that it became clear. Honestly I had forgotten about it just hours after Moon told me, I was focused on the Nestor situation. Seemed to me that years gone by is perfect circumstances to forget about me.

Furthermore would he not assume I was dead? I had been shot through the throat and last time he saw me I was laying lifeless under circling crows. I guess he knew that wouldn't be the end for me, after all it was he who first named me el hombre muerto.

On an afternoon after work at the bar just like many other days, I brought the name up.

"What is your relationship to Nestor?" After I spoke I lifted the beer bottle to my lips, like so many times before he and I didn't really look at each other. Delgado remained pretty tight lipped but did volunteer some more information about his own intentions, I suppose that is what I wanted to begin with.

"You are a brave man senior and a good marshal, I know what happened in Mexico and how Vincente felt about you. He was a great man, a great leader. Before you came no-one in Mexico would challenge him, he was untouchable. Congratulations senior, when you killed him you became the great man, a man whom nobody would touch."

I thought a while about what he said, I knew I would not be able to avoid it. Eventually, whether that's sooner or later we would have to kill each other and I didn't want to. I had learnt a bit about senior Delgado in the short time we worked together, he conjured fear, respect and obedience in all who faced him. I ain't never seen nothin' like it before.

There is a kind of unspoken law, some strange truth that I can't explain but I know it exists. The world of animals has a type of hierarchy, a heard of horses can easily be as many as a hundred but there will only ever be one stallion at a time. When a pack of wolves changes its leader, the new leader must kill the old one otherwise the pack is in disarray and the new leader will be killed. Either me or Delgado was like the old leader wolf and if it was me then I would gladly move aside so that he may be the stallion. It meant nothing to me to have a reputation throughout the west and south. To be feared, respected and admired impressed most men but I saw no value in any of it.

I was content with sitting out on the porch under the stars with a bottle of whiskey, a rocking chair and my girl. Delgado wouldn't allow that, the laws of men and animals wouldn't allow that and Purgeatory wouldn't allow that. As I sat contemplating the situation I felt sad and frustrated, I had accepted that I had to kill senior Delgado. I was sick of killing and the whole damned west with all of its primitive rules. Why couldn't we coexist, I didn't care about being the leader. There was always an alternative I could allow him to kill me. If I did that the town kept their new marshal, Delgado kept his life and I got to rest away from all this. I was tempted, honestly as I sat there I didn't know for sure what I would choose.

    It didn't happen for another couple of weeks but in the meantime there was a new resident in the house. Way out on the city limits I saw a dog. I didn't think anything else of it, there were lots of stray dogs wondering out there. On the way back to town the Mexican was moving his head a lot, it was like he was looking around. Turns out that is exactly what he was doing, the dog from the city limits followed us all the way back to town. He didn't leave for a few days but in that time he hadn't caused

any trouble so I didn't mind if he stuck around.
He would walk beside the horse and the Mexican seemed to be ok with it. He slept outside at night on the porch, there was good and bad points to his barking in the middle of the night.

    The town of Purgeatory had changed a lot in the past few years and had become a much less dangerous place. It was still Purgeatory. I kinda liked knowing whenever anyone came round especially in the middle of the night. Just a few days before the showdown with Delgado eventually happened, I came back to the house to find something that blew my mind. I had until then thought that impossible.

CHAPTER 30. A LEAVE OF MY SENSES.

Days just past had been hard for me, coping with loss is something I have become accustomed to. Despite that, it has been much harder than I hoped it would be. The day before the shootout with Delgado we had an exchange of words. It got a little heated, I guess I knew it would happen soon after that. We finished what we were doing and I locked up the marshal office, I knew that Moon and Maria had gone to the county fair so when I got back to the ranch me and Clancy would be alone. I took a slow ride home. Nice on a warm summer evening even if I spent the whole way back thinking about the imminent confrontation with Delgado, I decided whatever happened I had done all I could to avoid it. I had to accept which ever outcome transpired.

When I got back to the ranch I wasn't expecting anything, I had no reason to. The door was open but there's nothing unusual about that it was the summer, the house was cool if we kept both doors open. As I stepped inside I called out to Clancy she didn't answer but that didn't give me any reason to think something was wrong. When I got a little further into the house I saw blood all over the floor, Clancy was laying on the floor in the bedroom. She was dead but worse than that she had been mauled, I spent a short while with her and then searched the rest of the house looking for dog.

    I heard whimpering in the kitchen. At this point I was not in control of my state of mind, I found dog laying in the kitchen. He was alive but also hurt one bloody wound on his neck another on one of his legs, I was knelt beside him, he put his paw on my arm. I don't know what I thought, she was just through there covered in bloody wounds all over her body. Here he was also covered in bloody wounds but still alive just. Heart racing he was bleeding pretty heavy and breathing real fast, it seemed pretty clear to me what happened. Dog attacked Clancy leaving bite marks all over her, she must have picked up a knife and tried to defend herself then after he killed her wondered out here into the kitchen. I put my pistol to his head and put an end to his suffering after that I felt sick, I needed some air.

The kitchen had a door to outside, just outside I was trying to shake the feeling that I was gonna be sick. Couldn't get my head straight, just then I looked up and noticed something laid on the floor just off in the distance. I walked over there to see what it was, damn wolf.

Can't tell you all the things that were going round in my head, all the different emotions. I just about managed to stay with it long enough to work it out. The wolf came round and found the door open. Came in the house, that's when Clancy got attacked and either killed or died of her injuries later.

Dog must have been outside heard Clancy cry out and came running in here to see what was going on. The wolf ran out through the kitchen door probably the same way it came in, dog gave chase after it. The wolf and dog must have had a fight outside in the yard which apparently dog won. Then he came back in the house to find Clancy, for some reason ended up here in the kitchen where he laid waiting for me to get back here before he would die. Tough dog, killed a fucking wolf! Then laid waiting for me, he must have been in such pain. I somehow knew he was trustworthy and loyal, I just feel terrible that I ever thought he did this. I'm sorry dog!

    Maybe if Moon was here it wouldn't have happened, maybe if I was here or if the doors were closed. There are a dozen ways this could have happened differently but it didn't and I had recently come to thinking that things happen the way they're supposed to and couldn't have happened any other way. If dog was not here I would just have found Clancy dead on the floor and no way of ever knowing what happened to her.

    I knew as I stood in the yard looking down at that wolf, a few things were undeniably true. The first of many was that I had to bury these bodies, the second was I had to get rid of that dead wolf if I left it here other wolves would come looking for it. Also I had to tell Maria what happened here, to her sister. But the thing that was playing on my mind is what Moon had said a few days back, his father had given him a message for me. He said "when I saw the wolf I was to go see him." Had no idea what all of that meant then and still don't know and yeah maybe it was an incredible coincidence. But even if that was true, I found explaining the coincidence harder than believing somehow he knew this would happen. I could not vouch for my mental state and I admit I made a few mistakes, understandable I suppose.

    I left the house just as it was and took off on the Mexican. I think I had convinced myself that Moon's father suspiciously called Wolf, was gonna be able to help me make sense of all this. All the shit that I had experienced in my life, I just always put it down to people, this is how people are. This is the first time I couldn't explain it as human behavior, the first time that I could not blame it all on a person or multiple. This presented a problem for me, for the first time in many years I could not control the situation. I was angry about what had happened, losing Clancy and dog also angry at Moon for not being there. Was angry at Wolf, if he somehow knew this would happen and didn't tell me, then he is as to blame as anyone, I could have prevented it.

These years later I know that I was seeking for a human element for someone to blame because if I found someone I had a response. I would kill whoever was responsible for this, didn't care who it was. The Mexican kept slowing down, he knew where we were heading and didn't want us to get there, clever bastard. Each time he did it I kicked him and told him to get on with it, called him a lazy son of bitch. We did eventually get there and the first of the unrepairable relationship breakages was Clancy, the second and surprisingly the one that felt the most sensitive was dog.

I knew none of this was Moon's fault but I also knew every time I looked at him or heard his voice or even his name, I would keep thinking he could have prevented this if he would have been there. That was the third unrepairable breakage, it had occurred to me that maybe the Mexican would be the fourth. He wasn't somebody you treated that way. As I said before, he came to you or he didn't. It was his choice and if he wanted to leave, he was gone that's it. I seemed to upset him once before and he left, I thought then that I would not see him again. To my surprise he later came back and maybe that was a second chance he felt I deserved. After this night I was expecting him to leave again and I had no reason to expect a third chance, I know I didn't give them.

    When we reached the native village I sent him off calling him a coward. He said something back but not understanding horse, I'm not sure what. Whatever it was it was probably both equally unpleasant and well deserved! If you would have asked me then why I did that, I would have said I didn't know. Caught up in all the emotions and mad thoughts that were going around in my head or just angry, hurt and hitting out. Ask me now and I'll tell you the real reason was because as the saying goes you always hurt the ones you love, of course it's true. I sent him away because I didn't want to lose anything else I cared about, that night and because I knew whatever happened there I would regret later in life.

I was still just about hanging on to sanity but I could feel it leaving me and the madness getting stronger, after all you know my story! If anyone knows what the madness feels like, it ought to be me. So it seemed that I was going to be taking a leave of my senses for a while and just like before in that time, all bets are off! As for Delgado's bullshit story about from time to time there were people who were just wound up so tight no-one else would touch them, well that much at least was true. His idea that he had ever experienced such a thing before however, that was something that he was gonna learn real soon and it would be a lesson that would cost him more than he was willing to pay. It was Wolf, high chief of the tribe and Moon's father that was going to have an experience now however. If he didn't have answers that I liked, he was gonna hang while I ripped the skin from his bones.

CHAPTER 31. TO KILL OR NOT TO KILL.

I was of the mind to kill, didn't have much concern about who or what. Just as I pulled back the veil to the tent I saw Wolf sitting on the floor, there was no one else around. The tribal village was empty all but for him and me. He was burning some shit or other it stunk pretty bad, and at the same time singing one of his stupid songs. I wasn't fluent in the old language but I spoke a little, the song was about a burning spirit or some shit. He saw me standing there looking at him, didn't get up, asshole didn't even try to bargain with me. I wasn't available for reasoning with or appealing to, he just fucking sat there singing about ghosts and spirits on fire.

I pulled my knife and walked toward him as quick as I could but I never reached him.

That shit he was burning, whatever it was I walked right through the smoke and then the next thing I knew I woke up in the tent him still swaying back and forth singing. I tried to stand I couldn't, tried to find my knife and I couldn't. Felt like I was paralyzed, I just plain couldn't move. I could speak just about, I told him what was gonna happen when I got up. Was gonna sever his head, son of bitch didn't even look at me, just kept fanning the smoke and singing.

    Think I was in and out for an hour or so then I started to notice shadows, odd thing is as I looked around the room I didn't see any people. I had to get out of there. I swore to myself that I could at least crawl, I would be willing to crawl on my hands and knees in this particular scenario but just this one time. I did make it outside and the air started to help clear my head, bastard drugged me with that shit he was burning. I knew I had to kill him but he found a defense, I just couldn't get in there without succumbing to the smoke. Despite shouting him "get out here you son of a bitch" he remained unmoved. Time just kept on passing and I was getting nowhere but the hate and anger and pain wouldn't go away. I couldn't even get a moment just for clarity.

I had to kill someone or something, I could still see the shadows dancing around the tent.

That's when it hit me, son of a bitch knew I would be coming, he had protection. What else could I do but wrap my shirt around my face and run back in there, I fell to the floor again but this time I wasn't going to sleep. I was so close, if I could just reach out and grab him. I reached out toward him but it was no good, I could feel those things holding onto me pulling me back. Despite trying not to, I kind of had to accept I had lost and was powerless to do anything about it. Exccept just lie there and look him in the eye, he had tears streaming down his face but he wasn't crying just singing, fanning and swaying. Then he spoke but not in words and not without stopping singing, it was as if his body and his voice were in separate spaces doing separate things.

He tried to tell me, that's all he said. Maybe it was the hallucinogenics, maybe it was just my weak willed spirit. I don't know why but I just laid there and broke down. I cried out over and over, it went on for what seemed like hours. He didn't stop the whole time and wouldn't be swayed, just kept singing, crying and fanning the smoke. I eventually passed out, intoxicated from the smoke and exhausted from the emotion. When I awoke he was gone, the fire was cold. Even the ghosts had gone and I was alone. Always alone!

    I was numb, could not feel, could not think. It felt like I was learning to walk. I tried to stand and I somehow managed to stumble to my feet, wobbly still. I wondered how long I had been out and yet still feeling the effects of the smoke from those herbs. I moved the veil aside and stepped outside. It was still night and that didn't make sense as I'd been in that tent for what seemed like many hours. The village was still and quiet, where had they all gone?
I just walked off into the night, had no idea where I was going, just felt like I had to walk.

As I was walking the sun came up, in the light I noticed where I was and if I kept walking I would come by the town. The edge of the town outside the marshals' office, that's the moment I understood. Delgado, I had to kill Delgado.

  I was prepared for whatever would happen, one way or another the way this was going to end was with Delgado's body being displayed in the center of town for all to look at. Wish I could dramatize it a little more for your amusement but it just wasn't that exciting. I stepped into the office, the son bitch was sitting in my chair. I could feel the hate and the anger in my chest, it made me sick like my gut was twisted and I was choking. I looked at him a while, he just sat looking back at me. I watched his face change from one expression to the next, until eventually realization. I know well enough the look on a man's face when he knows he's about to die, I have seen it enough.

  He first sat forward, then stood up and just before he spoke I tipped the desk, grabbed the pot of coffee and hit him with it.

I just kept hitting him and there was no coffee pot left. My arm was shaking and my heart was beating out of my chest. I looked down at my hand and I couldn't tell which knuckle belonged where. He was laying on the office floor in the corner, I stood over him. Right now as I'm speaking to you I'm sorry and I'm ashamed but at the time I loved every part of it. I never felt so alive, all the lives I had taken; I never enjoyed it. That moment I did, I wished for him to still be alive so I could beat him to death again. I settled in the end for draggin' him outside, then I walked over to the saloon to get a horse.

  I tied the horse's rope around one of his arms, then went back to the saloon for another.
By now there was a crowd, no-one was saying anything, just staying out of my way which was wise. I tied the other horse to the other arm and sent them off in opposite directions, there was a post staked in the ground just outside the office. It was for tying horses, I used it for nailing the rope to it. Then I shot dead the horse on the other

side of the street, it was good enough to keep him on his knees but just about upright. I went to the saloon for a drink. Well now we know who the killer is and who is the prey. Good riddance senior!

CHAPTER 32. REMORSE.

The body hung there for a week or so, nobody would touch him. I took my breaks outside, I'd sit and drink my coffee with the decaying remains of a man I once knew. With regards to my team, I had not seen any of them for a few days. I hired them despite opposition from the city council, I spoke up for them when the good people of Purgeatory saw them as surplus to society's requirements. And now, days after I just disappeared, no sign of any of my deputies. They didn't come looking for me, they were not investigating the death of Clancy or my dog. They didn't seem to be interested in the murder that took place at the city marshal office. I was trying to decide whether to fire them or kill them.

The situation was confusing and left me searching for answers, as for the questions.

Well I was back to who am I again, who or what. I have been many different people so far in my life and I didn't like any of them. Wasn't sure whether I was ashamed or proud of who I was. I had taken so many lives and couldn't love, not properly. The question was not did I have anything to be ashamed of, the answer to that question seemed simple enough. More like did I have anything to be proud of, I spent a few days just walking around the wilderness. I tried to recall all the moments of my life so far, each memory I asked the question "am I proud of that?" After I don't know 2 or 3 days I guess, I came to the dubious conclusion that I was proud only of one thing. My enduring ability to endure, put another way I was tough.

    This environment bred tough people, it was a hard environment but even in the company of tough wilderness men. I was something on a different level. Most of the times that I had killed were men. That's not all, I had to be honest I had killed just because I could. Upon realizing that I was tougher than everyone else, upon realizing that so many had tried to kill me and none had succeeded an unexpected fault occurs. A misconception, an illusion. A singular thought, "I'm too strong to die!"

Must be a lie, no man can truly be too strong for death, even me. I supposed that if anyone was to genuinely test that theory, it was destined to be me. I seemed not to be able to die, speaking of misconceptions, a popular one was that I did not feel what others felt. This of course is not true, how could it be. The words that describe the pain I had felt were strangers to my vocabulary. Try as I may, I could not describe to you what the bullet that passed through my throat felt like or the hole that remained after. The snake venom coursing through my veins or the infection from drinking dirty water. Torn rectal tissue, 7 day hunger pains, bullets and blades. All I knew was pain, the conclusion I had reached was that the pain I had experienced had made me tough. True for all of us I suppose but in my case I had experienced more pain than others and it was undoubtable that I was tougher than others. Which forced me to draw the conclusion, the more you suffer the tougher it makes you. That said there is an idea that in order to endure anything truly devastating, enough to toughen a man substantially, he must first be strong enough to endure it. A vicious circle.

I was unaware of any reason that I would be so enduring, so strong.
I recalled at that moment what my father told me when I just a boy, seemed like so long ago now. "That which hurts us has a way of making us stronger."
He also said that, "only the strongest survive." It's as if he knew what life would be like.

Anyway, so here I am now as tough as it gets and left to wonder what the point is.
Is it just to endure, to ensure survival? Well if that is the case then I wonder what the point to survival is if there is nothing to survive for. What was I enduring a long pointless life for?
Just so I can get old and tell young people that I did it? It was the point to all this suffering and pain and enduring that I was

trying to find. My existence had been entirely pointless from my own perspective, yet from others, it was a legend. Easy for them to say, that have not felt the pain, the anger; the hate.

So, where would I go now? Could go back to the ranch but I didn't want to go there, maybe stay in town at the hotel or whorehouse. I could go off into the wilderness again, just like when I was a boy. None of those options appealed to me. I decided to stay at the city marshal office and wait for the team to show. The following day came and went but there was no sign of the team members. More interestingly there were no calls either, a whole day had passed and the office had not been given any work.

The second day confirmed my suspicions, they all thought I had gone mad, that and they were all afraid of me. I suppose the corpse outside the office didn't help matters. The following day I approached the undertaker to resolve the Delgado situation. He acted different to what I had been expecting. The same at the saloon and the whorehouse. A week or so after the Delgado incident, I was forced to come to the conclusion that the relationship between the town of Purgeatory and I had come to a permanent end. There had been no work for a whole week, no sign of the team for a whole week and I had not exchanged words with anyone other than the undertaker, the barman and a whore named She.

    I knew very well what happened to people this town didn't like, was kind of waiting to see a team appear in town with one purpose in mind. The thought kind of made me sad, as I had been the one they trusted with that work for so long. To think that they might hire others, strangers to resolve the problem that this time was me, was a deeply sad thought. I couldn't say for sure that I had not succumbed to the madness of it all. I could not say for sure that I was still ok.

CHAPTER 33. THE BEGINNING OF THE END.

I was packing to leave town, for good this time.
I had a horse waiting for me outside, I had planned to leave quietly without causing a fuss.
As I stood there tying up the saddle bags, I couldn't help but look up at the courthouse.
I somehow just knew they were all sitting in there talking about me, watching me.
Sometimes I just get caught up, I get carried away. This was one of those times, I didn't plan to but I just looked up and as soon as I did I couldn't help walk up there.

I busted through the doors and they were silent just waiting for me, just looking at me.
I wanted answers, wanted to know why they turned on me. Tried to explain that I was confused after what happened, was hurt.
Nobody seemed to be concerned about that,

their lack of response was getting to me. Things went from bad to worse pretty quickly. I thought the situation was about to blow up. Sgt Green was the only one to approach me he talked, that's all, just talked. I didn't take a lot of convincing to leave town, had planned to all along. At some point the Sgt mentioned that they all understood why things went bad. He admitted that it was common knowledge Delgado was in town to kill me, it was always gonna be him or me.

    Then he told me something I hadn't thought of before, the only survivor of that mass slaughter in Mexico. Nestor, it had to be Nestor. That was all the convincing I would need to leave town, I was fixed on Mexico and the job I had to do. I think I kind of convinced myself that finishing that piece of business would give me peace. I didn't know it at the time but I should have, there is no peace and there never will be. I used to think that I might lose my mind and then convince myself that it would never happen, I was too strong for that.

By the time I left the town of blood heading for Mexico I knew. It was slipping away, so now what? Was certainly not prepared to give up and just let go of what makes me civilized.

I know I am not going to win the fight but that does not mean that I just give up. Never lost before and I didn't know how I would react to losing, what it would be like. I was concerned that I might not be honorable in defeat. Tell you the truth, being strong was never that important to me, it was necessary. I was only ever concerned with being honorable.

I had now lost everything I ever loved, in a way it was now too late to try to hold on to anything other than honor. Along the long path to Mexico I happened upon a camp, Hopi I think although it was never confirmed. I was crying when I met their scout, was a foolish act but I kept riding towards him once I had seen him. I rode right past him and did not draw a weapon, I know it was a mistake and I did not care much for the consequences. I was captured, not much of a surprise.

At first they just beat me without asking any questions, I didn't mind. I felt that the beatings were honest. If I didn't complain or cry out then I was honorable. A few days passed then a new face appeared, he was an angry man. You can tell a lot about a man by looking in his eyes, this was a man full of hate. He had a lot of questions to ask but I don't know what they were about, due to not being familiar with their language. I think he broke my eye socket, I'm not an expert on these things but I couldn't control my eye when I wanted to look to the side or down.

As the conversation progressed I lost sight pretty much completely out of that eye. I could even see with my other eye how much swelling there was. He put a blade in my side, felt like between 2 ribs. He left the blade there but I was grateful that it was a clean blade at least.
Eventually he brought a translator in, I was still crying but not because I was in pain. The translator called me by a name I hadn't heard before, Crazy Bull. It was a name that I would hear a lot more in future. Seems all

they wanted was reassurance that I wasn't scouting their territory. They set me loose but it was a curious event, I cried a little more then walked off.

There were many men and women standing as I was leaving but no one said anything.

It was a child who ran from the comfort and safety of his parents, I turned when I heard them calling out. He approached me, I turned toward him, another mistake. Then a hunter from among the village shot an arrow at me. They don't miss, the boy seemed more concerned about me than himself. He was trying to give me a blanket, the bow man took aim for another but one of the elders stopped him. I took the blanket from the kid and went about my business. I was trying to stay with it but I just couldn't stay on my feet, the world was spinning then I fell.

When I woke, I was back at the Hopi villiage. I did not know what to expect, I had supposed it would be more violence, shouting and questions. My suspicion is that the new approach was an attempt to get me to relax enough that I would divulge something new, something that I withheld during the previous interactions. A day or so went by and they treated me pretty well in that time. A girl had been coming by to give me water and she cleaned up my eye and ribs pretty good. We hadn't spoken, she tried a few times but kept looking over her shoulder toward the door. I thought that might be because she was afraid of being caught talking with me. Which would mean it had been forbidden. One time, she came to the tent sobbing. Was usually me doing the sobbing and her just attending to the wounds.

    I could stand now but I still needed help, I had to stand to make water. She helped me stand and then just stood looking at me, I didn't know how to tell her what I was trying to do.
Anyway I was heading for the door. When she noticed I was going for the door, she rushed over and stopped me. So still a prisoner then. Well, when you gotta make water you gotta make water. I turned my back to her and went over in the corner of

the tent, would have preferred to go outside but maybe some other time.

    Not much else to do but lay back down, she came over to help me and well I fell. Pulled her over, she landed on top of me and just for a moment she lay on top of me looking at me.
As I looked into her eyes, I couldn't help be aroused a little. I mean it had been a while since Clancy and I had laid together. She rightly got up and left, I swear I was just about to kiss her.

    So I figured I hadn't been eating for a while, I had been beaten a lot and of course lost a lot of blood. Added to that, they used to come in at night and wake me for a beating so sleep was hard to come by. I was obviously confused and not thinking clearly, wasn't even sure where I was. All night I laid awake thinking about that Hopi girl, thinking how I wanted to kiss her. I'm not sure even now if it was a dream, a hallucination or if it really happened. She walked in, in the middle of the night and dropped her dress off her shoulders.
Beautiful sight, a naked woman standing

right in front of you. So the only thing I was sure of is, it was obviously another tactic. I mean they beat me for a week, they didn't get whatever they were after.

Then they switched to being nice, still not satisfied with the lack of answers. So I must be one of those men who open up to a lover, especially right after or during sex. Fair assumption however, knowing that I didn't know whatever it is they wanted to know.I just decided to take the sex and worry about the answers in the morning. Besides, not even sure if it was real anyway.

      Still have no idea who she was but she was lovely, a lovely woman and I was very fond of her. Not sure where it came from but I had the idea that upon sunrise I was just gonna leave.

The lovely girl left some time in the early hours, I fell asleep right after we got done. Haven't slept so well in months. I guess that considering no-one had come into the tent in the time since she left, there was not to be any repercussions. I was just hoping she was ok.

Sunrise woke me after I had slept better than I can remember in a long time and I felt actually pretty good. Stood up and went to the door, after I pulled open the curtain and looked outside I saw them all standing there. Looked like what must have been the whole village.
Nobody said anything, they hardly even moved, kinda surreal actually. Again not sure if it was even real, it was as if they were clay models of people made to look like real people placed there to trick me. I stepped outside then pretty much just got on with it, I didn't have a horse here so I had prepared myself for a real good walk. We talked a little before about unexpected events, well this was another.

A ways past the statue villagers, an elder stood just off to the side stepped toward me.
As I got closer to where he was standing, he stepped in my direction again. I stopped when he stood in front of me, wasn't sure where this was going so I didn't speak just waited. There was always a thought that I would get so far and then they would stop

me and drag me back. He instead offered me a horse which I gladly accepted. The real surprise and the real gift was I noticed a tear leave his eye and migrate southward down his old troubled face. Have no way of knowing what it means for sure but I like to believe that it was because he didn't agree with what the villagers had done and knew all along I was not a threat to them. Just a poor madman passing through from nowhere to somewhere else that lead nowhere.

    He stood and looked at me hoping I would take the horse, hoping I would take the apology and be about my business in peace. I want to believe he was looking for forgiveness for his people and reassurance he didn't need to continue to worry about this. Truly I was touched by this and shed a tear also. I was hoping that as we looked into each other's shiny glass like eyes, a single nod would suffice. I myself was reassured when I could see his face change, a look of relief and another. Maybe the other look was a childlike response to being rewarded with the reassurance he was

looking for, his eyes didn't look quite so sad anymore.
I felt good about that and will remember his smile all my life.

CHAPTER 34. COYOTE STEALS FIRE.

Not too long ago I was back there at that native camp, been thinking about that a lot these past few days. They treated me pretty rough and I have killed many for much less, yet I bared no hard feelings against them. I had been questioning this, what was the difference between what they did and all the other men I have put in the ground over the years. Curiously there was a part of me that was, well I don't know if I'd go as far as to say grateful but certainly I was glad of their harsh treatment. Sounds like something my father would say but I dare say it that kind of treatment is almost cleansing.

In the same way that the good town of Purgeatory is cleansing as in dividing all men into two main groups. Those who can't bare the pain and despair and those who can. It's no surprise to me that I was among the latter group. Even so that is not all. The other part of it is that all men have to atone for, some more than others and I know I have indeed much to atone for. That experience at the native camp felt like I was atoning and that somehow gave it a meaning, felt like there was a reason for that brutal treatment. I think that is the key, I knew I had it coming that I deserved it. Even that still doesn't say it all, there was another element.

I also was aware that anytime I could have ended it, could have killed them all and there was nothing they could have done to prevent it.

    If you ask me now, I know that some of them were wise enough and old enough to know that too. Like the old man I spoke with just before I left. I didn't need to prove any of it, not to myself anyway. Enduring that kind of punishment because you have no other choice, there is nothing you can do to stop it. Is not even close to being the same as enduring it because you choose to, though you can end it at any time. I felt in that moment that I was atoning and obviously that is what I wanted to do.

Strange thing now is that I feel somehow enlightened, or that I have left behind a weight that had been draining me of energy, trying to drag it around with me everywhere I went.

      Somehow I had missed the pain, or maybe not so much the pain but the challenge of it.

I will try to explain as best I can, suffering something is unbearable, hard even when there is no choice but in some ways it's even tougher when you can stop it. There is a challenge at a time when suffering pain, punishment or despair. The challenge is how well you can take it and how much you can take, this was my specialist subject. When I was a boy, I was helpless and had no choice but to endure, that was a hell of a challenge for me as I recall. Answering that challenge felt impossibly hard and I often believed I could not do it. Having proved myself wrong many times, I had grown tough, as tough as they come. I hadn't previously realized it but I had been missing that particular challenge for a while. The quest for this reward system was a constant endeavor, never truly being satisfied. I knew I would always need that, it defined who is was.

Even then I felt like I needed to be tougher, needed the challenge and the reward.

I rode a little through the night, it was cool so didn't bother the horse and I couldn't sleep anyway. We rode across a camp, fire still burning but no-one around. No one except a coyote that seemed somehow intent on picking up one of the burning logs with its jaws, despite the obvious risk. I watched him as we rode by pretty sure he got burned a few times, still kept going back. That is what I've been talking about, the coyote was just like me. He too felt he had need to improve. He had need of this reward system I mentioned briefly a little while back. The nature of animals is un-spoilt out here not at all like our own. It is the natural way to get burned then to respond by building a fire. I never said I understood it.

There are many things I wonder at night when I lay looking up at the night sky, full of stars. Often I think about the

Mexican, Mimi, Dog and Clancy. Also I think about that mad bull my father had all those years ago, my mother and father. What became of their ranch, from time to time I think about the coyote and think "I wonder if he ever got where he was going." Maybe he died set a blaze at that campfire or maybe he's still there now, still trying to catch flame with his jaws or steal fire. For the most part I was done with gun work, done with fighting for causes. I had learnt that was a business for young men.

    I can say happily that I had grown out of that business, but still I have need for the challenge. So where now do I go and what is next for me? Questions that I know only I can decide the answers. Maybe I would became a bandit, an outlaw. Didn't seem to suit me much robbing trains and seizing trade caravans or small strongholds. I swear by my very blood and bones I will never work for the city again, never soldier for the good of the country again.

    The concept had eluded me previous but no more gladly, for a man to fight for a way of life or a political agenda requires him to hold it in regard. I wouldn't ever fight to save the world 'cause I didn't think much of it the way it was, a little change would be a good thing.

I cared not whoever won the war, the north or the south, made little difference to me. Reason being because I would never work for either of them. Eventually I fell asleep and at some point during the night I dreamed of the coyote. Still trying to steal fire with nothing but its jaws. I admired his attitude, was much like my own had been many years ago. I had been feeling for a while now like I had it easy, everything going my way. Was city marshal and that paid pretty well, had a house, a woman and even a dog. What business has a man like me with such things? I was like that coyote. I was designed for the struggle, the challenge and my only gratification was the reward system. To say "I lived while all others died, I survived what all others could not" was the only thing that ever really felt right.

    I had been wondering whether what happened back there had been my fault after all.

For trying to have so much, I have always known that the universe works in its own mysterious way. For everything a payment must be made. It seems right as I look back now that having so much would indeed require a hefty payment, much like the one made by Clancy and Dog when the wolf came to collect. I didn't want any more of that kind of thing and felt renewed by the realization and the intention to go back to what I know. Just being out here struggling to survive, never knowing what life was gonna throw at me next. Every day almost dying then finding a way to endure, to live on till the next challenge. That was what I knew, that was what I wanted.

    I awoke from that sleep feeling better than I had in years. Recharged and clear headed, just me and no one else around. No friends, employers or employees. No woman or dog to care for, I even let the horse go, sent it away first thing. This felt so much more natural to me, my stomach was empty, I was dry as a bone and I had nothing. The way it should always have been.

CHAPTER 35. ONE LAST JOB TO DO.

Mexico, Nestor. My last compelling thought, the last thing I had to do to be free of it all.
So I had been on my way there for a good while now and by this point wasn't far away. Kept thinking about how it was gonna play out, there was an old part of me from before that kept trying to think of tactics. That was not how it was gonna happen. I said before, I was to be free of it all. All that I had learnt, the experiences that I had and the impact they had on me. I briefly mentioned before, "the way it should always have been" and that is how it would be when I got there. Just natural, just me. Was past time I got back to that.

Hard to recognize landmarks and places but I was sure I was going the right way and of course on foot this time. I knew when I got there I would be straight into it and I accepted there would be no plan or tactical maneuvers.   Had to assume that Nestor would have the whole town manned although I would have one thing in my favor. They could not have known I was coming, not sure that would be much help however.

As time passed I come to accept that there was a good chance I would not make it out of that town alive and I felt at peace with that. I also thought that I might die before I got even, that I was not at all comfortable with. So the objective was clear, I would kill Nestor. Didn't much care about the rest of his men or whatever state the town would eventually be left in.

The whole point of this was Nestor, like tying a loose end to prevent it from further unravelling.

I was betting on a couple more days walking and I would be just about there, then probably before I made it to the town, would be picked up by a scout party.

I suppose honesty is the best policy, I got kinda enthusiastic about the prospect of dying there. Story was a great one but has to come to end eventually as all good stories do. And of course would have to ensure that it would be a fitting end. I had no desire to go on, nothing left to achieve and nothing left to fight for. Had no plans or desires for the future, so may as well just let it go. Found an area with some berry bushes and decided to stop there for the night. Those berries were good eating and I had my fill as dusk was descending over the land. That night when I made camp, there was no fire, wasn't gonna alert them to my presence. I slept pretty well but not at all in comfort but after a full day of walking I could have slept standing up.

    The following morning I came across a trail in the sand by the looks of 2 horses leading a caravan pulled by 2 more. I saw a high point just up ahead, so I deviated off to the left to get up on it. I looked down over the valley below and I could see the caravan loaded with barrels of whiskey and other supplies by the looks of it. If it turned out to be guns, I would have sacked it but as it was, seemed like little point in destroying a supply caravan. It had its use though as far as I was concerned, couldn't really be heading anywhere else but there. I just followed it at a distance for the remainder of that day, they never really looked behind them as far as I could see.

Just about before night fall we hit a small outpost, I could see the town just off to the distance, no more than half hour walk away. I walked right past them, didn't say anything just stood in silence watching me go by. I continued into the town and met with a bastard, didn't concern myself with the name he went by. He spoke of warnings and postured over the seriousness and dangerousness of him and his friends. Clearly he was impressed, not so much by me though which made a nice change. Can't say how long he spoke for but it seemed like a lifetime, I waited patiently for him to get done. Eventually he shut up so I took my chance to retort, didn't really want to speak with him and didn't have a lot to say.

It's a good job I did try to speak with him 'cause he broke some news that I was not expecting. I had spent so long thinking

about Nestor, about what I'd do, what I'd say.
Well you could try to imagine how surprised I was when I heard the son bitch was dead. So naturally I switched to thinking that it was all a tactical move, a lie. Seems that whatever agenda I had previously imagined was as far from the reality of what I would find there as you could get. I would get my fight anyway as it turned out, the town had been taken over by a rival gang from a neighboring town. They stormed the town not long after I left the first time I was here, after they had learned of Vincente's death. Nestor had taken over from Vincente naturally, he was killed when the new occupants arrived due to him being in command.

These new serious and dangerous people didn't permit tourists and wouldn't allow me to ever leave that town alive or dead. The first thing that came to my mind was how perfect that was, it would be inconclusive whether I died there or not. Many who learned of what was inevitably going to take place here would believe that I perished like so many others who made the mistake of visiting this town under the new regime. Body burned or cut up and fed to the wolves, maybe buried out there somewhere in the vast expanse. No doubt others would argue that and say "no, he's out there somewhere", "there's no way they killed him, can't kill him" or "he's too strong to die." So this was it, the best chance I would ever have of the perfect ending to a great story. Then as I heard the squeaky wheels of the cart rolling into town behind me it all became clear. This is how it was always going to be, the final chapter all along.

Nothing I could do or say would change anything now.

There was another cart outside the building that used to be the saloon, now like all the other buildings in the square, empty. Well empty except for the bandits taking up firing positions behind the windows. Another group on the roof of the same building, didn't look behind me, didn't need to. I knew what I would see if I had. No head count this time, the legend was ridiculous and I would feed it no more. I thanked him for his warning but was quick to point out that I was gonna go for him and to hell with the consequences. His face changed, don't they always. I saw all the gunmen he knew that, I realized I would probly die in just a few moments and he knew that too. Yet still, I was gonna go for it and he was first.

    We looked each other in the eye a little that was only ever gonna end one way. As he started backing up I started out after him, well he was almost at the door to whatever building it was he first came out of when I caught him. Just moments before the shooting had started and mostly they hit the ground around me. They left it too late anyway, I was heading toward the building so half of them would lose whatever angle they had bargained for and the others would have to contend with the building providing some small amount of cover. Whatever happened I had heard enough.

    As he reached for his gun he tripped on the first of several steps, an obvious disadvantage of walking backwards. Hadn't reached for a gun myself yet, I stomped his face a few times.

Hadn't planned it but he was laying on the ground looking up at me with the familiar pathetic expression of a man who had realized he wasn't what he thought he was but I was. That drew a conclusion to our business.

I headed inside to conclude negotiations with the men in there. What I really needed was fire, nothing quite cleanses a town like fire.

After working through the small group inside, I went back out to the street. I was pretty quick but I still took a few hits, nothing fatal. Not yet anyway. The plan was to send the alcohol cart over to the other one, the gun cart. I just about managed to turn the horses and sent them off in the right direction. Their aim improved dramatically apparently. It became clear to me that I would go no further, I just needed to light the fire and I would be done. Fortunately I had the presence of mind to bring the matches that were on the table in there with me. Those and a document I found on the table in there along with the matches.

Lucky for me I also removed the little wooden cork from one of the barrels. After I lit the trail of alcohol that lead from my location to the carts. I just laid back in the sand dying.

Not surprisingly the gunmen had stopped firing shortly after whichever of them was the smartest, had figured out my plan. I can only assume stopped firing so that they could focus on running away from the cart. I could hear sounds of shouting and the squeak of the wheels as they travelled towards their target. It seemed like I was waiting ages for the cart to reach its destination. As I recall I was just about out when I eventually heard the explosion. Mission accomplished of course, I never doubted it.

CHAPTER 36. THIS IS THE END!

Every human regardless of gender or age or color has to be properly integrated into society. However you may feel about society and believe me when I say that I understand, why would you want to be part of it? What we call society is so obviously lacking in any kind of virtue you can relate to, a seemingly conscienceless society. Also I have noticed that so it seems at least, there are those of influence and not necessarily power because that would imply they are in a position of power.

There are those of influence who take increasing steps into a consequence free action, therefore not too much of a stretch to imagine that a society or culture without consequences would be fertile ground for themselves and those so inclined. My prediction, if you are reading this, is that in the future they have already shaped the world to suit.

In my time a man can point a gun at another man and fire it and kill the other man but before you go thinking that is consequence free. Allow me to point out that at any moment a man or woman, even a kid can point a gun at me and fire it and kill me. So one might argue that the consequence is that whilst there is no mechanism to protect others from me, there is also none to protect me from them.

The rather obvious consequence therefore of shooting a man is that his brother or father or son is likely gonna do the very same in order to obtain revenge. This simple observation is a thing I know, only too well to be true. So what is different about my view of the future is that those people who seek to create it have only one agenda, which is very obviously to get away with their actions without having to suffer retaliation.

The men here are bastards there is no doubt but even among the bastard class there are those who would not shoot at a man without a gun. It is inevitable I suppose that some men are too weak to take on a man in a fair one on one with no obvious advantage. Interestingly but not surprisingly those men are the ones who live. The brave, decent men who hand their opponent a weapon before setting about their destruction, invariably don't look forward to the same kind of life expectancy as the cowards do.

As it is in my time now, there is not yet a law against defending one's self. Retaliation is still legally permitted, escalation is frowned upon and unprovoked attacks are unacceptable.
The worst thing of all is for someone to attack another far weaker than they are themself.
A great example of this is when somebody beats on a whore. I do absolutely detest that and I am by no means the only one who cannot tolerate that.

Another good example is when a bunch of men turn up at a ranch unexpected and uninvited and the only one home is a small child, unprotected and all alone. These things are unacceptable.

Those men are often brutal and declarations of war should be only the very last resort as they are likely to never offer or accept terms of surrender or peace and will fight to the death.

They have their faults and I have put many of them in the ground but they tend to and not always, have honor.

The most brutal and dangerous men I have faced, I can think of three in particular, were decent towards whores and decent towards women in general. This has been my point all along, a strong man is a killer there's no doubt about it. But his victims are the dishonest and dishonorable.

Every man, woman and child must be properly integrated into society. The consequences of failure to integrate are simple and are best understood by observation. I know myself that my path is result of failure to integrate. What I find intriguing is that those who are properly integrated have no notion of this, are oblivious to the concept even. The moment my mother died my path was chosen, nothing was gonna change that. The moment father died was the very moment I was set on my path without option to leave it. Then finally when those bastards came to the house was the moment I became aware of it.

Time for a different thought. At some point in the future, every man and woman will have to think about whether they have to act in order to preserve whatever is left for the future.

For the next hundred or so years people will just serve themselves. Their whole lives will be about what they want only. They will gather unto them what they want to be theirs. Without any concern regarding the cultural or legal situation of the environment they live in.

At some point people all over the world are gonna have to take responsibility for the men they raise. That's gonna be made more difficult for that generation by the failure to do so of all the previous generations, including their own parent generation. I watch people, I can't help it and sometimes it doesn't occur to me that I'm doing it. Everybody is the same, their needs are the greatest needs. That's untrue, think about it. Can't be true.

The whole human species is, (serve yourself).
Everybody thinks the same way, who is going to clean up our environment for us. I wish I knew how to convince people but I don't. I swear to you this is the truth. Long after my bones have turned to dust, you will all still be fighting the same troubles and stresses that people in my time are fighting. You all need to change the way you think, I implore you whole heartedly.
Just listen to me for a moment, give me one chance.

If everybody remains the same then the worldwide environment remains the same.
Remaining the same of course means getting gradually worse, If everybody says and does whatever they want, thinks and acts however they want then they ensure the world stays the same. It wouldn't be hard to change, all it would take is one generation. One generation to say, "what serves me measured against what serves the world around me." That's all. No-one's asking you to live a selfless life, giving everything

to everyone else and having nothing for yourself.

Another way of looking at this, politicians get a pretty bad name. I don't think anyone likes politics or politicians. Every politician has a few things in common and they're undeniable. Greed, corruption and a conflict of interest. So put in a way that you may relate to, would you like it very much if self-serving greed and conflict of interest was removed entirely from the business of government? We all would. But it is true also that you all, yourselves do the same thing. Self-serving greed is the fault in the human species that threatens to bring about its end. Until we all stop, the human race has no future.

I surmise that the only way a species has a future is what you might call a hive mind.
Each individual brain, heart and body thinking, feeling and doing whatever benefits everyone equally, mutually. That is whether you like it or not, whether you accept it or not. The way the human race was always supposed to be and if any of you

want an easier or more rewarding or fairer existence or even just want a future, then that is the way it has to be.

    Whatever your personal feelings, which I agree you are entitled to, they do not in any way modify the truth as it pertains to you. We each of us are absolutely responsible for the world around us however miserable or great you may find it. I'm sure you will be pleased to know I'm gonna take a short break from these observations to tell you about something I heard a few years back.

36.25. ERROR! NOT FOUND.

At one of my many trips to various native settlements I heard a shaman tell a tale he held in some high regard. Unfortunately I cannot remember where I was but I do remember the shaman. This tale was legend to him, he was telling a younger man about this legend. I get the sense it had been dear to him for as long as he'd been a shaman and also it sounded like it wasn't just to him but to all of his peers as well. There are a few different groups of shaman in this area three to be accurate. The old man was of the Shikaaree Pakshee. He would say they are the most respected, I'm quite sure a man of another group would say the same.

The Shikaaree shaman was by his own admission apparently the most accomplished and well respected of his group having been a student and close friend of his master, Master Nilam or Neelam I'm not too sure. Master Nilam or Neelam was long dead by the time I heard of him but ask any shaman of any of the three groups and they will not only know who he was but have nothing if not admiration and respect for him.

I asked around a little at the time, he was apparently almost 100 when he died and that was somewhere around 60 full cycles of the seasons ago. The shaman I'm talking about, Master Muk'Tarr himself must be nearly 80 years. And he himself like Neelam before him, considered to be the elder on all matters considering anything affecting all the shaman, regardless of their group name or color.

Muk'Tarr started the tale talking about his friend and mentor and the good days they would spend studying and trying to read what he calls akashik. Akashik being a full record of everything that ever has and ever will happen. Every thought every living being ever had and everything they ever felt, a full and complete accurate history of everyone and everything, everywhere since the beginning of time till its end.

Neelam was looking for his master Ten Buk who disappeared sometime around 220 full cycles ago, 50 years before master Muk'Tarr was born. There was no trace to follow, he simply was there one day and gone the next. Muk'Tarr around 30 years or full cycles ago was asked to help a farmer who had land in the mountains along the western coast far south of here. The farmer had tried several other shaman who were all unable to help and some refused even to try. Muk'Tarr was the name he had repeatedly heard. The farmer's problem was according to Muk'Tarr a mine on his land which had been discovered when clearing wild bush from the entrance, which was marked in some foreign form of writing he said the farmer later was told it was Mayan.

A tall doorway in stone was entrance to the foot hills along a mountain range, with the Mayan writing along the top of the doorway. It had been stoned from the outside and then covered with wild thorn bush, the Mayan was clearly trying to hide the entrance. The farmer had opened the entrance after what looked to be a long time judging by how well established the wild thorn bush was. He sent a small team of young laborers into the mine to inspect the interior, they did not return. He himself refused to go in there stating that whenever he was near he had terrible feelings.

A nagging voice of despair in his mind and thoughts of mutilation. Muk'Tarr travelled the long road to the farmer's land and when he arrived at the mine, he said he could clearly hear a voice but not a human voice. And not with his ears but instead inside his own mind. Muk'Tarr said he left shortly after stating he had to take his time to prepare. He made a make shift the camp outside the mine. He remained in the camp outside the mine still on the farmer's land but along the edge, he said he couldn't sleep for the wailing of the mysterious voice. He could hear the voice constantly the whole time he was there and he thought it intended to force him to lose his sanity.

After a few days his mind was subjected to images, unwanted horrifying images he would not say what the images were. After a week he said he couldn't prepare any longer, as the spirit responsible for the invasion of his mind was threatening to break his mind and take from him any memory of who he was. He entered the mine instructing the farmer to not let anyone else enter under any circumstance, no matter what was heard. He also told the farmer to get everyone else off the land and sell if he could, if not to cut his losses and just leave.

As Muk'Tarr reconstructed the events of that day, his skin turned pale white as he spoke of it. He went inside and the voice he had been hearing began to threaten him. Warning of what would happen if he came any closer. He said he knew what was happening and what needs to be done. Almost an hour he walked, trying to find the spot where the body lay.
The mine twisted and turned and after a short while Muk'Tarr realized that the mine had been built from a cave.

A vast ancient cave system that seemed to stretch over a very large area. The original mine builders must have been advanced as it was very old but still the mine looked workable. There were many branches off the main path and he tried lighting torches along the way to light the path but also to mark where he had already been. Some of the entrances to side paths had large cobwebs across them. He said that he tried to stay on the main path but did go a little way down some of the smaller paths only to turn back when the walls narrowed.

    He hadn't found anything yet, other than discarded tools which looked old and worn. There was no sign of the body of along the way. At a sharp bend in the cave path, he could see that the miners had stopped building the mine as there were no more wooden frames of the mine workings beyond this part of the mine. He walked around the bend carefully as it was dark and difficult to see even though he held a torch. The shadows on the walls danced by the light of the torch and they were eerie. In the dancing light he could make out a structure up ahead, it was a door. When he opened the door in the dim light of his torch, he saw a large room. He entered the room and in one corner he could just see what looked like a torch.

He knew that was the place but also he had a realization. He was not the first shaman to tackle this spirit. There were wooden bowls with clumped dust covered in cobwebs.

He read as best he could the signs of the other shaman's work, and came across a letter penned by someone claiming to be Ten Buk. Ten Buk who had disappeared 220 years ago.

Master Muk'Tarr came to the conclusion that master Ten Buk had been called in to help with the problem by whichever previous land owner. He had spent time preparing in that very room but seems he had sadly met his end there.

At this point in his recollection of that day's events, he had not yet found Master Ten Buk's body. He read the letter Ten Buk wrote, addressed to any other shaman who might end up there. Clearly detailing the events that led to his tragic death. He arrived there and found a mine entrance that had been covered by Mayan shaman almost

1000 years before he had arrived there, according to the writing above the entrance. Master Ten Buk was familiar but not fluent with old disciplines of language, Aztec, Mayan and Incan.

The Inca originally worked the mine that they say they found when exploring the area for resources, they tried to work the mine and had problems. They offered the mine to the Maya who refused to purchase it. After that the Inca abandoned it at a loss but hired reputable Mayan shaman to try to clear or clean the mine. I can only imagine what was meant by that.

The Mayan shaman where killed and disembodied in the mine and never returned to the surface. At this point the Inca who were in the area had gone and the remaining Maya laborers engraved the archway above the entrance and in an attempt to cover the entrance they planted thorn bushes right in front of the massive stone doorway The engraving was a warning, roughly translated. "Do not enter this mine under any circumstances. There is nothing within but death. No living soul will be spared."

Or something similar although I'm sure far more eloquent.

After something near 1000 years a native man found the entrance and tried to uncover it.

He hired a team of laborers to uncover the entrance and open the mine, it took almost a year. After opening it he sent a team to explore and a few men returned stating that there was something terrible in there and they absolutely would not under any circumstances return to the mine. "I, Ten Buk, shaman was hired to investigate and if possible clear the mine of whatever inhabited it."

I have spent almost one week here and I now know I will never leave. My mind is not my own. Learn from the preparation I have done and save yourself, spend no more than a few days here at the most. There is a spirit here, it's old very, very old. I don't know what it is, my mind has no frame of reference to offer me explanation. Whatever it is, it's very old and I'm sure now that it never was human. I cannot say how long it has been here or where it came from but I have learnt that destroying it is not within the realms of possibility.

At best it can be starved, it becomes weak when it is starved and perhaps if it becomes weak enough it may simply cease to exist although I cannot say for sure that even this would be possible. Its nourishment is the fear and suffering of its prey. Misery, despair and desperation.
It needs humans and animals to come here, I found a small mountain of remains some of which I could not identify. Some bones were clearly human and some were clearly animal but there was some others that I do not know what they were. The remains I found, I tried as best I could to bless and to free from this place. I ordered them removed from here.

It's like the afterlife here, I feel all of the spirits here, all of the victims. There are so many I cannot count them. Sometimes I can hear them, they recount the last thought of their final moments. Everyone died in fear and despair, they beg and plead and try to bargain.

It laughs at their desperate fear. I have a plan but I'm not sure it will work. If you find my body beware, it is not mine any longer. I died here.

I have no idea if it can animate a corpse but I have seen some things down here that I do not believe to be possible and can only be explained by the impossible. It seems that whatever it is, likes to play with remains of its victims taunting their spirits after death by making them watch their bodies self-mutilate. I don't know if it enters the body or just animates the body with its own energy. I am relying on another to come here someday and read this note.

Find my body and set me free. I am going to feed this thing my body in the hope that I can trap it within.

It will take all the spiritual strength I have to fight it for all these years. I cannot promise that I will but I promise I will try. If I succeed all you need do is destroy my body and if I'm right it should cost this thing whatever it is, its energy also. Like catching a flame in a jar, smash the jar and the flame will be destroyed. You must destroy my body.

Well, I would say that the tale is along the border line of the fantastic but Master Muk'Tarr believed every word he was saying. He found Master Ten Buk's body and according to him it was indeed animated. Which of course is impossible for Master Ten Buk was presumed dead 220 years ago. His body would be rotted and decayed by then.

Master Muk'Tarr says there was a fight between him and Master Ten Buk. I have heard from other shamans that when they have been preparing for a battle they do not eat or sleep very much, but instead take wortweed. I also know that too much wortweed smoke inhaled in a space without much fresh air can cause hallucinations, especially when searching through dusty, dark and eerie caves or mines.

I think Master Muk'Tarr had been burning too much wortweed, but I will never know as he swore that his story was true. In the end Master Muk'Tarr managed to burn the corpse of the long deceased Master Ten

Buk and take the remains outside the mine. He removed them from the land all together and sent him to the ocean. I don't know how much of that is true or even if any but I know one thing for sure. Ancient native shaman legends are fascinating stories.

36.5. THERE CAME A BEAR!

There is another old tale that I'm aware of. Regarding a young woman, she lived apparently alone in a cabin in the woods. In town a man saw her leaving the doctor's office alone and followed her home. She had noticed him following her and decided to act against the man before he had a chance to do whatever it was he had in mind. She rode not to her home but instead to an abandoned cabin not far from her own. He did indeed follow her to the cabin and he watched her enter and close the door behind her.

He stepped onto the porch and knocked the door, the first time there was no answer but he waited. The second time there was no answer and still he waited. There third time there was an answer, he heard the woman's voice from inside the cabin, "it's open." The man opened the door and stepped inside, he noticed a huge figure in the corner of room. He harrowed his eyes in trying to focus on the figure curious about what it was. He said hello and asked if there was someone there. Just then something on the floor caught his eye, he looked towards it. The woman was laid on the floor under the bed. As he looked at her he was preparing to speak, she just looked right at him but said nothing. Then the figure in the corner of the room moved and caught his eye. It was then he identified what it was.

A large hungry bear. He turned to flee and made it outside the cabin but was caught and mauled on the porch. The young woman waited until the bear had left and ran out the door to her horse and rode away quickly not looking back to see.

Some years later an old native man found the cabin and the body on the porch, Dr Rosen.
Assumedly he had gone after the women to answer her call for medical treatment. The woman got scared and presumably misread his presence and led him to his death. The native traveler also found three other bodies all men. And a very old bear. The cabin

was in no habitable state even without the bodies that littered the floor. There was no sign of a woman but there was already by that time a legend of a young mad woman who was a bear charmer.

She had been leading people there for years, as far as I know there were no other doctors so maybe she had not misunderstood the other men's intentions. There was a, maybe best described as very much in the realms of the fantastic tale surrounding the story after that, which still is told now. Some cowboy decided to start the rumor that the native man, the traveler who found those bodies is the bear.

He was cursed by his own brother for trying to steal the affections of his brother's beloved. The curse was in the nature of beastation, the brother would be a lone beast feared by all, especially young women, more often than he would be a man. The story was later changed to say that he knew he was a beast man but he covered it up claiming that he found the bodies as a way to try to hide that he had been responsible. The reason for doing that is pretty clear.

In order to avoid reprisal.

36.75. FULL CIRCLE.

Do you remember way back at the beginning? I started telling you my story from the exact spot where I am still laying now. I started talking about my mother and my father and about when I was a boy. So as we reach the end I am still just laying here under a blanket of stars. Kind of a cowboy and kind of not at the same time. Part native and part white American. It's probably accurate to say more creature than man.

This then is how it is to be for me, I will live out here alone. I find food every once in a while. Hunt with my hands. I build fires. There is a part of me that finds comfort in my freedom. No home or employment. No responsibility or relationship. Not even a horse to be concerned for. I am as free as a man can be in the modern world as it is now, in my time.

A life without chains and anchors yes, true.
I must also acknowledge that it's a life without meaning or purpose. Years from now I'll be older and maybe that will change my mind. As for now at least I am without care, without concern regarding the nature of my meaningless life. Regarding my nature.

For all I have done and all I have accomplished. All I have made and saved. I have also destroyed as much. Taken life, scared people and taken ownership over them.
No one is good, at least not in my time. There are people who do good things and there are people who do not. No one is good, regardless of what they do.

At times throughout my story maybe you think he is a good person. This is a man of conscience. Conscience, yes. Maybe at times you thought I was honorable? Well, that I am.
Also I have humility and empathy. Sure it sounds like I am a good man.

Also though, I am mad. I can be as callous as anyone. I do not lose sleep over the people I have killed. At a time, I can kill or worse without remorse. I can choose not to feel, compassion, empathy or mercy. The truth is I do not know what I am. My feelings, my humanity is on a switch inside my head. A switch that I have complete control over. I can be pleasant and courteous and I may save your life one day.

Also though, I can be inhumanly cold and I may take your life one day. Best thing all round I think is just stay well away from me and I will try not to hunt you. When you young men hear tales of my life and think you know who I am, do not come looking for me. In the words of a wise and highly evolved being, "don't go looking for snakes, you might find them!"

I will smile at you with arms wide open and bite into you at the same time. Ask yourself why I live way out here alone? I stay away!

My hope is that you too will stay away. You will die if you come here. I am the one who walks among corpses of those who were my enemy and those who were my friend. I am the one who waits for death to come for me and yet he will not come. When you wander out too far and you begin to smell the decay and the death, when you hear the echoes of the cries of the dead from the afterlife; when you see the dark sky overhead and the stale air lingering in front of your face and you feel the cold chill your skin. Turn around and walk away.

    Walk, never look back and pray to the gods if you believe in them that I may spare you and they may protect you. I have been named Crazy Bull. My mother used to call me Small Bear. In the tongue of her people I am known as the one who is wild. I had a white name but it has been so long since I heard anybody use it that I no longer know what it was. Most recently I have been called simply, Wild Bull. And this is how my story ends.

BIO

Too strong to die is not his first novel but will be the first to be published. Books have always been close to his heart and it has been a dream to be a recognised author since childhood. Having a parent author has been a constant source of inspiration. He has always seen both the spoken and the written word as almost magic but has struggled to master it due to a combination of Autism and Dyslexia.

As for the story itself, unlikely as it seems, he insists that this story is not at all fictional but instead a man's life. A man who whilst dead for many years spoke to him as a spirit and told of his amazing story. The author therefore feels that he was merely a conduit for the man to tell the world who he was and how he lived, so that he is not forgotten.

There will be 4 special first edition hard back printed copies. These will be numbered on the spine, 1 – 4 and after the Book has achieved its best success, they will be auctioned with the entire proceeds going to a registered charity to be determined.